to mé rodině

That's a three-part rule of mine: (1) never complain about a situation while the situation is still going on; (2) if you can't believe it's happening, pretend it's a movie; and (3) after it's over, find somebody to pin the blame on and never let them forget it.

ANDY WARHOL
The Philosophy of Andy Warhol: From A to B & Back Again

Where once people turned to fiction for plot and character, drama and action they now turn to the filmic or televisual.

ELIZABETH YOUNG
quoted in *Shopping in Space*

I sure as hell didn't want to look like Jackie Kennedy.

MARILYN MONROE
quoted in *The Last Take*

Marilyn's Almost Terminal New York Adventure

JUSTINE ETTLER

PICADOR
Pan Macmillan Australia

First published 1996 in Picador by Pan Macmillan Australia Pty Limited
St Martins Tower, 31 Market Street, Sydney

National Library of Australia
cataloguing-in-publication data:

Ettler, Justine, 1965–   .
Marilyn's almost terminal New York adventure.

ISBN 0 330 35780 8.

A823.3

Typeset in 10.5/13pt Sabon by Midland Typesetters
Printed in Australia by McPherson's Printing Group

Also by Justine Ettler

The River Ophelia

Justine Ettler was born in Sydney in 1965. A graduate of Sydney's University of Technology, she is currently completing a Ph.D. at Macquarie University and planning a third novel.

Her first novel, the bestselling *The River Ophelia*, is also available in Picador.

Acknowledgements

Thanks to: Jan McKemmish, Una Ellis, Andrew Serling, Amanda Brown, Tony Charleston, Gaby Naher, Linda Funnell and my family.

Lyrics to Elton John's 'Candle in the Wind' are reproduced with kind permission of Music Sales Pty Ltd, © copyright 1973 Dick James Music Limited, c/o Polygram International Music Publishing Limited.

Contents

this story about Marilyn doesn't start with her moderately immaculate conception or with her depraved adolescence with its idle daydreams about becoming a movie star and moving to Hollywood or with that summer she spent clinging to a bobbing beyond-the-breakers surfboard off Australia's most famous beach and squeezed orgasm after orgasm from between her tanned teenager's thighs.

In this story about Marilyn our brave heroine is heading for Manhattan and this story starts when she's standing in Sydney's Kingsford Smith departure lounge waiting to meet a girlfriend who's already a couple of hours late and Marilyn decides that if Virginia deeply-enigmatic-in-a-very-James-Bond-girl-way Woolf doesn't turn up in the next five minutes she's going to board flight Q03 to Honolulu and LA without her.

All passengers for flight Q03 to Los Angeles now boarding from Gate 12.

And just as Marilyn thinks how typical it is of Virginia's too enigmatic deeper self to fail to appear like this at the last moment she notices a familiar form in a tweed coat and denim lurking over near a row of empty vending machines and in a blinding neon flash of colossal magnitude she recognises hairy snail—

Oh God now I'm going to miss the plane—

in this story about

Marilyn our brave

heroine is heading

for Manhattan

Lawrence as he glides towards her and all her bags across the yawning expanse of the departure lounge.

Oh shit.

And when Lawrence sees that she's seen him he starts to glide faster and faster until he's actually running so Marilyn makes a desperate grab for her bags and tears off for the gate.

But Marilyn's only halfway there when she hears a ripping sound and looks down just in time to watch all her carry-on luggage spill out onto the white lino floor and as the I-haven't-slept-properly-for-I-don't-know-how-long tears well up in her eyes Lawrence is suddenly right there beside her gathering up all her things and throwing them into a giant-sized plastic airline bag and saying:

'Have fun with Virginia OK? Oh and don't forget to ring your mother you know what she's like any excuse to dial "E" for emergency,' all eyes like a possum and serious hairy snail concern.

And Marilyn smiles through her tears and then Lawrence says in a passionate husky voice she's never heard before:

'Bye Marilyn I'll miss you,' and kisses her tenderly on each sticky wet cheek.

And then Lawrence winks and cocks his finger like a gun and propels her through the gate with a gentle shove just like a B-grade actor playing a flawed hero in a low-budget third-rate Hollywood Disaster Movie and Lawrence's image is so terminally infested with white noise and is so many generations old that its highly suspect genealogical origin threatens to become sheerly and utterly untraceable at any minute in a random and incalculable way and as Marilyn blows goodbye kisses she

wonders behind bleary eyes who Lawrence is and why
he's a hairy snail and what he's doing waving a
goodbye that's so overcome by unidentifiable multiple
wave interferences and of such poor is-there-something-wrong-with-the-satellite-dish quality it's almost
unwatchable from the other side of the gate.

marilyn's still puzzled about who Lawrence is and how he knows about Virginia and how all this ties in with Twentiethcentury Fox and what's wrong with the picture on the small portable TV screen inside her mind and how all of this relates to her allergy as she leans back in her lots-of-extra-leg-room-emergency-exit seat and she's glad to be strapped in and anchored down because gradually the last couple of days drift back sporadically as people stumble in and out of the hazy blur and it's a little bit like coming out of a deep sleep and holding on to the last part of a dream and when the plane pulls away from the terminal she realises that if she's going to work out what she's doing on the plane at all she's going to have to go back to the beginning and make some kind of list of names and places before she forgets everything completely.

So Marilyn digs around in her giant-sized plastic airline bag until she finds a purchased-just-prior-to-departure now-I'm-going-to-keep-a-travel-diary notebook and just as she's gulping down her second deep breath of crisp newly starched paper an air hostess suddenly appears and grabs the bag and the notebook and angrily shoves them under an adjacent seat and while the plane completes its preparations for take-off Marilyn leans back in her seat passively pissed off and exhausted and it isn't until the plane is speeding down the runway that she thinks:

Wow.

And then she murmurs:

'Whoever said

an air hostess

suddenly appears

flying with a hangover was a problem?'

And as the wheels fold into their rectal cavities and the plane tilts eastwards Marilyn drifts off to sleep in a humming place of no dreams.

But that's when the air hostess noisily returns smiling this I-don't-care-if-I'm-a-lousy-hack-air-hostess-because-I-know-I'm-Bette-Davis-where-it-counts smile and offers Marilyn her giant-sized plastic airline bag back and sweet liquids and crunchy things and an airline-logoed biro on a little doily'd dish and Marilyn takes out the notebook and writes the first name in the list of names and places which is:

Lawrence.

But then she crosses this out and writes:

The List of Names and Places.

And then she writes:

> *This story about a young woman doesn't start with her moderately immaculate conception or with her depraved adolescence with its idle daydreams about becoming a movie star and moving to Hollywood or with that summer she spent clinging to a bobbing-beyond-the-breakers surfboard off Australia's most famous beach and squeezed orgasm after orgasm between her tanned teenager's thighs.*
>
> *This story about a young woman starts when she's sitting at a desk in a crowded office in front of a word processor counting the hours of emptiness and drudgery until lunchtime and the woman's thinking that she doesn't want to spend New Year's Eve*

*with hairy snail Lawrence and she wishes
that new and exciting things would begin to
happen and as she wishes about new and
exciting things a cold bolt of adrenalin
rushes through her body and she's sure
something's going to happen soon and
then when she's out on her lunch break
she runs into my-wife's-spending-New-
Year's-Eve-in-the-country Miller who asks
her back to his place after work for a
couple of drinks and when the young
woman returns to her desk in the crowded
office everyone's already popping bottles
of champagne and so when she arrives at
Miller's flat her face is flushed and she's
already a little drunk and she feels as if
new and exciting things are beginning to
happen and they do.*

Marilyn thinks this is a good way to start her remembrance of things past although she's not sure whether to skim over what happens at Miller's or not because looking back it all seems so tacky but she can't help thinking that *The List of Names and Places* is infinitely more fun than anything she's ever done before and so what if it's tacky so she continues with the bit about Miller and writes:

*Miller lives with his wife and baby in a
cramped one-bedroom inner-city flat with
too many books and records and a bed
covered by a piece of batik that is now a
couch and as they sit together on this*

batik bed-couch it's not long before they start to do all the things people do when they have lusted after each other for a long time and it all starts with Miller talking about her eyes as he takes her hand in his and then as he goes on to trace the blue and delicate veins up the soft and white as porcelain flesh of her forearm the young woman is glad that she had the half bottle of champagne at the office because she's feeling pretty uptight as she stares at the snapshot of Miller's family and when she tries to moan Miller's name in his ear it comes out mumbled stumbling over spit-drenched lips in an incoherent I've-never-done-anything-like-this-before rush but Miller doesn't notice because he's just thinking how great it feels to have this blue-eyed girl with what he imagines to be a very liberal yes-I'm-yours attitude moaning incoherently in his ear on his batik covered couch because he thought he'd never go through with it and then all of a sudden he does and everything's over in an explosive things-will-never-be-the-same-again rush and Miller sort of blacks out for a few minutes in a murky messy love stung quagmire and meanwhile the I've-never-done-anything-like-this-before-but-does-it-mean-I'm-finally-living-in-the-fast-lane? woman reads bits from the newspaper that's scattered on the floor and then checks the time and says:

8

'Miller I've got to go.'
And as she leaves Miller takes her
phone number because he wants to do it
all over again before his wife gets back.

Marilyn rereads the first few pages of *The List of Names and Places* which is a little like running the last few hundred metres of a marathon and as Marilyn's breath comes in gasps and her heart begins to pound and the sweat begins to drip into her eyes she realises that hairy snail Lawrence is the man she's just spent the last three years of her life with and recently betrayed by starting an affair with someone called Miller and that's when Marilyn flops back in her chair and lets the notebook slip down into her lap and mumbles something like:

'Oh my God oh my God.'

And then she closes her eyes and tries to calm down and says to the sleeping American in the next seat:

'You know Lawrence there's this one Sunday afternoon that stands out in my mind in bold colours as some kind of turning point in our relationship and it's late autumn and we're lying around in our little flat with the silvery wallpaper and red carpet after too many chocolate croissants and coffee and I'm feeling full and very content and I ask you if you'd like to go out for a walk or for a drink or to see a movie or do something and you're just lying on the carpet with your eyes closed and you say:

'"Let's just have a quiet night at home and watch TV."

'Remember?'

The sleeping man mumbles:

'I'll have a pastrami on rye with butter and a little tomato and a few of those pickles and some lettuce look forget the pickles and give me some mustard yeah hot mustard great and some potato salad yeah on top of the lettuce no? OK on the side and a large coke no ice.'

And Marilyn says:

'And for a minute I don't say anything because I'm in shock and then it slowly dawns on me that it's never going to work with us Lawrence because we're just too different and you never take me or my allergies seriously and that's when my throat starts to itch and my eyes start to water and my nose is running as I say:

'"You know I can't watch TV because of my hay fever Lawrence we've been living together for two years now and I haven't watched TV in all that time because the radiation and negative ions or whatever make me sneeze for days and all the sitting around waiting for something to happen makes me nervous and even talking about it is making my eyes water."

'And then I sneeze a couple of times and you just roll over and turn on the TV and then I slam out of the flat and stomp down to the park and sit on a bench and sulk all loneliness and despair and think about all the times you've made jokes about my allergy to TV in front of our friends at dinner parties.'

Then the sleeping man says:

'Could you make that a diet coke? OK and some of those French fries on the side but hold the catsup yeah that's all thanks and you have a nice day too actually have a nice life OK?'

And then the sleeping man groans and rolls over and when Marilyn opens her eyes the air hostess is hovering around her seat listening and when the air hostess notices Marilyn's eyes are open she starts fussing around with oodles of aren't-we-doing-a great-job-here? efficiency and charm and an open bottle of chilled dry white wine which she slaps down in front of Marilyn with a plastic cup on a doily'd dish even though she doesn't give Marilyn anything to eat and as she walks away Marilyn thinks:

She didn't give me anything to eat and I'm hungry and confused and I wish I could work out what day it is.

And then she thinks:

This air hostess must be the worst air hostess in the world and no better than a lousy hack pretending to be an air hostess and I wonder how she manages to keep her job on one of our famous flying kangaroos?

And just as she thinks this the air hostess reappears with what looks like a tray of food and as she rearranges Marilyn's table she slops a bit of wine on the sleeping man and when she finally does slap down the tray with one of those mullet-at-dawn flip flop slaps Marilyn sees a pack of children's size playing cards on a doily'd dish and a packet of cracker biscuits rendered inedible by their very ingredients and a satchel of powdered milk and says to the sleeping man:

'I can't eat any of this.'

But the sleeping man doesn't say anything and it seems to Marilyn's covetous eyes that everyone else has been rewarded with mountainous steaming piles of salty reconstituted kilojoules and it's with a jagged desultory six-hours-flying-time confused sigh that Marilyn decides to take a break from *The List of Names and Places* and puts the notepad and airline-logoed biro on the tray and pours herself a glass of the no

11

longer chilled dry white wine and thinks of Twentieth-century Fox.

And it's a little like coming out of a deep sleep and holding on to the last part of a dream because Twentiethcentury's face has become a little fuzzy around the edges and seems a little featureless and Marilyn can only vaguely remember his beneath-the-appearance dishevelled self and the jaded world-weary look about his face but even this tiny smudge of memory is clearer than the terminally out of focus smudges of Miller or Durrell or Lawrence and thinking this she can't wait to meet Twentiethcentury Fox in his apartment in Manhattan and it's well into the third glass of wine that Marilyn decides to take up pen and paper and add creative-director potential Durrell and hairy snail Lawrence to *The List of Names and Places* because she doesn't want Twentiethcentury to meet her in this shabby disorderly state and conclude that she's one of life's lost little square pegs without a square hole or a round hole or even a clothesline or any other purpose in life so she writes:

> *As soon as the woman gets home I-can't-get-you-out-of-my-mind Miller rings her and says:*
>
> *'I've got to see you again.'*
>
> *And as soon as the woman hangs up the phone from talking to Miller the phone rings again although this time it's hairy snail I'm-having-a-drink-with-Durrell Lawrence who wants to know where she's been and when he can come and pick her up and she makes up a lie*

*about being held up at the office and at
that moment a car full of yelping dogs
drives past the open window and the
woman struggles to stifle her mounting
hysteria until she hangs up the phone.*

*And later that night she meets Durrell
who has the perfect doing-a-couple-of-
lines acquiline nose of a first-class sommelier
and while Durrell does a lot of talking to
Lawrence he simultaneously showers
several sunny smiles on the woman who
watches his nose distend and contract
alive alone and naked on his face while
the phatic discharges keep pouring forth
like a constant stream of oncoming traffic
from his full Botticelli lips until finally
Lawrence and his polite disposition go to
buy some cigarettes and suddenly she's
alone with Durrell and that's when she
notices his hand on her thigh as he says:*

'You have beautiful eyes.'

And the woman says:

'Thank you you have a great ass.'

Marilyn knows she didn't say this but she wishes she had.

*And then Durrell reaches across the table
and says:*

*'I'd like to go out with you some time
you know and have dinner.'*

*And that's when the third campari hits
her between the eyes and she forgets all
about Miller because all she can think*

about now is Durrell but as soon as Lawrence comes back Durrell goes home and then after Marilyn and Lawrence have dinner they go back to Lawrence's place and the woman sort of forgets all about Miller and Durrell because Lawrence is lying on his back like a hairy snail and she can't help thinking that he has eyes like a possum and that she probably loves him very much and may even marry him one day.

And that's when Marilyn realises in a falling star flash that deep down she really loves Lawrence but she wants to be absolutely sure and that's why she has the affairs with Miller and Durrell all in the space of two days because Lawrence's jokes about her allergies have filled her with doubt and confusion and nail biting anxiety.

Atchoo.

And even thinking about TV makes her eyes water and her throat itch and her nose run and she still isn't sure how all this fits in with Virginia and Twentiethcentury and the picture on the TV screen inside her head and thinking this she sinks back in her chair stunned and brainless and drifts off to sleep in a humming place of no dreams and she wakes up with a start as the air hostess slaps down another bottle of chilled dry white wine and a clean plastic cup turned upside down on a doily'd dish and smiling a lousy hack air hostess smile she drifts down the aisle with Marilyn's notepad in her hand although Marilyn doesn't notice and just pours herself some more wine and opens the pack of children's size playing cards and shuffles them slowly as a shadowy profile of Twentiethcentury Fox wanders around her mind's eye.

Marilyn is still wondering about the colour of his eyes and hair and skin and the details of his impeccable does-he-really-work-in-Wall-Street? business suit when the air hostess locks herself inside one of the tiny toilet cubicles and reads Marilyn's *The List of Names and Places* and the first thing she reads is:

Lawrence.

Which is crossed out and the next thing she reads is:

The List of Names and Places.

And then the air hostess goes on to read all about the young woman at the word processor and thinks that:

This story doesn't start . . .

Is a stupid way to start a story but she rushes on to read more anyway because at any minute there could be a knock at the door and she'll have to emerge pinkly embarrassed with a notebook in her hand.

And as she reads all about Miller she can't help thinking that it all happens very suddenly and she's also annoyed that it doesn't explain who Miller is or how the woman knows him and she thinks it's all very tacky especially the bit about Miller's wife and baby and 'hairy snail Lawrence' seems a strange way to describe someone and as she reads on she finds it a bit far-fetched when Durrell asks the woman out seeing he must be Lawrence's friend and no-one's ever done that to her but then she has to admit that the woman *is* very attractive in a very blue-eyed blonde-haired big-busted kind of way:

Very Marilyn-with-a-touch-of-Meryl.

And the air hostess feels very sorry for Lawrence and decides she'd like to meet him one day but she

15

can't help wondering if he really exists or if the woman is making it all up and thinks:

I'll just take a closer look at the woman and see if she looks like the kind of person who'd make all this up because I've got to find out whether it's true or not because of Lawrence and because if it is true then it means I've led a very boring sheltered existence for a glamorous air hostess who's really a budding actress.

And this possibility threatens the firey molten rock core of her very being.

meanwhile Marilyn puts the children's size playing cards back in their packet and falls asleep in a humming place of no dreams.

When the lousy hack air hostess sneaks back with Marilyn's notebook she fixes Marilyn with a searching gaze and traces the intricate shapes and patterns of the lines on Marilyn's face and attempts to develop a character physiognomy from the juxtaposition of Marilyn's pretty features.

But then—

Slam—

The lousy hack air hostess slams down a cup of white coffee with one sugar and tilts Marilyn's chair upright with a jolt and hovers around all flaring nostrils and smiling vaguely.

Marilyn opens her eyes slowly and shudders at the proximity of the lousy hack air hostess's face and gulps down the coffee all in one go and wills the air hostess to go away with thoughts like:

Go *away*.

And:

Get lost you creep.

And:

I expected more from our famous flying kangaroo.

And the sleeping man says:

'Oh Lois not now I'm asleep I'm tired Lois let me have a few more minutes just a few more minutes please?

the plane circles

Honolulu restless

and predatory

17

Lois let me go back to sleep.'

And then the air hostess leaves.

Meanwhile the plane circles Honolulu restless and predatory which makes Marilyn feel confused and anxious so she seeks comfort in *The List of Names and Places* and picks up her pen and writes:

> *The next day Miller rings as soon as she arrives home and the suddenly hungry woman agrees to meet him for breakfast where she watches the crumbs around his lips and the crumbs on his shirt-front and the crumbs on his fingers and then Miller mumbles something through the crumbs about coffee at his flat and the woman's still watching the crumbs as they hop onto the batik covered couch and do everything all over again covered in crumbs and this time the woman doesn't think 'I've never done anything like this before' because she's thinking:*
>
> I never want to do this with Miller again.
>
> *Although Miller is still turned on by what he imagines to be her very liberal yes-I'm-yours attitude and the afternoon passes in its own sordid nights-in-Berlin fashion and pretty soon the I-can't-stand-being-here-much-longer woman says:*
>
> *'I've got to go.'*
>
> *And Miller invites her to stay the night in a wheedling voice the woman finds very easy to resist because Miller wants to do it all over again before his wife gets back*

and as he watches the woman getting dressed he can't help thinking a corny post-coital commentary like:

Touching the soft downy hair around your belly button with my warm protruding moist bottom lip is better than a thousand espressos and stimulating coffee house chats with any of my extremely well-endowed coffee house buddies and infinitely more consequential than Schoenburg's invention of twelve-tone serialism or the downfall of the Whitlam Government and I wish I could be a great and masterful painter just for an hour so I could capture for posterity the curve of your hips that runs all the way from your head to your toes which I'm sure you're aware of and caress the sheer provocation of your perky protruding breasts with one delicate sweep of my brush and freeze for all eternity the honeysuckle sweetness of the afternoon light as it dances down your shoulders and back as you laughingly turn to face me with your very liberal yes-I'm-yours attitude and if only I could capture it all in a neat top forty pop song or in a three-minute video clip I'm sure that my wife would understand why I can't seem to think of anything else but the next time I can unbutton your shirt and do the things people do when they've been lusting after each other for a long time despite their mortgages marriages and families.

*And just as the woman is closing the
door he mumbles another post-coital
phrase that has something to do with the
bluey green explosion of stars and the cold
shuddering intensity of inevitability as
galaxies collide and the woman says:*

'See you later Miller,' and leaves.

*And as soon as she gets home the phone
rings and she knows with a cold pang of
certainty that it's Miller so she just lets it
ring and ring and as soon as it stops ringing
she rings Lawrence and Lawrence says:*

*'I just tried to call you but no-one
answered.'*

And then Lawrence says:

*'I'll be over in half an hour to pick you
up OK?'*

*And as the woman hangs up the phone
she starts to suspect that something has
begun to eat away at the solid rock foun-
dations of their three-year relationship
that has nothing to do with TV or allergies or dinner parties and it's with a
quickly sickening heart and a blood stopping sense of windswept inevitability that
the woman pours herself a very cold shot
of Russian vodka which she drinks down
in one just-like-Faye-Dunnaway-in-Barfly
gulp before pouring and gulping a few
more until she finds herself lying on her
bed undressed and unshowered and drunk
when Lawrence and Durrell and all their
creative-director potential ring at the door.*

20

And meanwhile it's become quite dark in her inner-city flat with the gas leak and it's almost as if New Year's Eve has begun in earnest because Lawrence and Durrell seem rags to riches transformed in their dark expensively tailored yet quirky dinner suits and Lawrence's eyes seem to dance and stare shinily like the eyes of a possum framed against his lemon polka dotted hand-tied silk bow tie and the wet pearly gleam of his neat Macleans teeth and the woman thinks:

Sweetie-pie Lawrence.

But that's when she realises that she's drunk and naked and unshowered so she invites them in for some Russian vodka while she disappears into the bathroom to make herself beautiful.

And soon they are all drunk and dressed and showered and this time it really is like New Year's Eve has begun in earnest as they stumble out into Durrell's black BMW in the rain like three fairy penguins lost on the high seas on a stormy night and as the woman watches Durrell's smudge of blue eyes shiftily savouring all her exposed flesh in lots of quick snatchy glances she begins to hope new and exciting things continue to happen and they do.

And the sleeping man says:

'Don't Lois please don't take advantage of me when I'm asleep come on leave me alone.'

And the woman notices that whenever Durrell shifts from neutral to drive he glances at her suggestively and the woman imagines Durrell's unspoken passions which probably have something to do with sensually intense sexual encounters and she can almost hear him moan:

'Oh I'm coming I'm coming am I too soon?' just like Lawrence used to do.

And the sleeping man says:

'Don't Lois oh please don't oh Lois oh yeah Lois yeah,' and starts moaning and writhing just another would-be Superman in his chair.

Although Durrell doesn't say anything at all and snatches another blue-eyed smudgy glance and the woman smiles from the corners of her wet lippy mouth as the windshield wipers groan through the warm throbbing intensity and when Lawrence says:

'We're here,' the woman just snorts softly and everything steams and simmers and while Durrell opens her door and Lawrence waits with his Missoni umbrella a strong sense of change hangs around in the evening air as tangible as a raindrop.

marilyn likes the sound of 'a strong sense of change that hangs around in the evening air as tangible as a raindrop' and thinks that it might even come pretty close to being poetry with all the 's' sounds and the melancholy poignancy of the image of the tangible raindrop although she admits that it never really happened at all and that it is something she just made up and that apart from coming pretty close to being poetry it's also nothing more than a thinly disguised attempt at underlining with a bold black pen the sense of inevitability that seems to be the only link between one list in *The List of Names and Places* and another and she almost crosses it out because how can three people simultaneously share a sense of inevitability tangible as a raindrop while they're standing in the rain as New Year's Eve begins in earnest? but something indescribable holds her back so she leaves it in and goes on to write about Durrell's party which is what she's wanted to write about all along and much easier to transcribe than any raindrop-like frozen moment of pseudo-psychic tangibility.

a strong sense of

change hangs

around in the

evening air as

tangible as a

raindrop

And the party is just like most parties with its loud music and atmosphere-adjusted lighting and there are a lot of people crowded into a small space who are dressed in varying degrees of up and down and at varying stages of progressive inebriation and having conversations that are loud sometimes interesting and probably inconsequential revolving around what everyone's been doing and where everyone's been going and who everyone's been screwing and what drugs everyone's been taking and where everyone's been on their latest trip to Europe and everyone's making vague misunderstood comments about art and misleading plot oversimplifications of the latest piece of celluloid to emerge from Hollywood and earnest justified theoretically situated ideologically sound comments about the latest piece of obscure new New Wave alternative cinema they just happened to catch on a quiet weeknight at a suburban revival house and some people are making witty and amusing small talk that amounts to nothing at all and the young woman finds herself alone in the middle of all this sipping and spilling her jolly Bolly from a chilled flute and sampling delicately flavoured scrumptious little luxuries from the all too prevalent catering service agency staff who circulate with just the right mixture of subtlety and charm chatting to guests and offering tray after tray of niceties and there's Durrell looking over as she sips spills silly singing to the record of Ella and Louis doing Porgy *and* Bess *as the traffic roars down Macleay Street.*

And after the fifth glass and the umpteenth silly conversation she moves over to the long trestle dining table and laughingly sits on a hard chair and Durrell sits down next to her and Lawrence sits on her other side but she's talking to Bronte who says:

'New York is just wonderful at Christmas with all the lights in the trees and the colourful displays in the store windows and we had a very romantic time walking around near Central Park holding hands and going ice-skating at the Walloman and falling over and I've still got bruises on my knees and you meet the most amazing people there because their attitude is so different like the time just a couple of weeks ago when we bought a Christmas tree and carried it back on the subway and we'd just bought it at this grocery store in Alphabet City from this Chinese guy and we'd just knocked him down in price from $45 to $30 without the stand and we carried it between the two of us through the six o'clock crowds in Astor Place to the station and we took lots of photos of each other holding the tree under all the lights and in the mushy snow and every-

thing so *anyway we carry it down into the
subway and pay our tokens and lift the
tree over the turnstiles and this very well-
dressed oldish businessman says:*

'The tree travels free?'

And we laugh and say:

'Yes.'

*And he sort of helps us to turn it
upright and get it onto the train and then he
says:*

'You must be from Ostralia.'

*And we're pretty amazed that he got
the accent right away and all we can say is
yes and anyway it turns out that he's a
film producer who's produced lots of
Australian films although I was a bit put off
by the fact that he thought that* Crocodile
Dundee *was only a harmless fairytale.*

At which point the woman says:

'Oh.'

And Bronte continues:

*'Anyway I think you'd love New York
and you should definitely go there sometime and I also think New York would
love you and you'd have a great time and
meet the most amazing people.'*

*And the woman nods and smiles as a
tall thin woman with a beaky nose and a
long lined face and a very creased linen
suit walks up to Bronte casting what looks
like a hot hate stare at the woman but
isn't and Bronte says in a voice squeaky
with suppressed excitement:*

'Virginia how are you? What have you been doing? You're looking wonderful tell me what you've been doing.'

And then Bronte's voice disappears into Virginia's shoulder and the woman smiles blandly as Virginia and Bronte wrap each other in a very friendly embrace and Virginia slaps Bronte on the shoulder and Bronte almost bites her tongue off in dry-mouthed surprise and then Virginia says:

'How was New York? When did you get back? You look wonderful you must have had a great time tell me all about it it really is so good to see you.'

And Bronte says:

'We must make an effort to see more of each other,' all gushy enthusiasm.

And the woman gets so sick of the way they're carrying on that she almost chokes on her mouthful of champagne and spits it out straight across the table and that's when she starts coughing and can't stop and her glass spills all over the trestle table and then Bronte introduces her to Virginia and Virginia slaps her on the back and says:

'Nice to meet you.'

Which only makes the coughing worse.

And then Bronte says:

'I was just telling her all about how wonderful it was at Christmas with all the lights in the trees and what a romantic

27

time we had walking around near Central Park holding hands and going ice-skating at the Walloman and falling over and I've still got the bruises on my knees and you meet the most amazing people there because their attitude is so different like the time just a couple of weeks ago when we bought a Christmas tree and carried it back on the subway.'

And at this point the young woman is in a real panic because she doesn't know if she's ever going to stop coughing and then Bronte won't have to shout so that Virginia can hear her because between each cough she manages to lift her watering eyes just long enough to notice that everyone is listening and watching as Virginia continues to slap her back but she can't stop coughing so Bronte keeps on shouting about carrying the tree home on the subway and in sheer desperation the young woman grabs blindly at a bottle of wine and guzzles it right in front of all the staring party people and as it runs down the front of her black linen dress into her cleavage and down her stomach she feels like she just might drown and when she's sure she'll pass out if she doesn't stop guzzling to breathe she hears Bronte say:

'Anyway I think you'd love New York and you should definitely go there sometime soon and I also think New York would love you and you'd have a great

*time and meet the most amazing people so
why don't you two go together?'*

*And Virginia stops slapping the young
woman's back and fixes her with a serious
permeating gaze and says:*

*'We should definitely do that some
time.'*

And the young woman replies:

'Sounds good to me.'

*And that's when Durrell puts his hand on
her thigh.*

And that's when the captain makes his announcement
that strikes everyone across the face like a wet rag:

'Ladies and Gentlemen,' he begins and goes on to
gargle something unintelligible about an unforeseeable
unfortunate delay and an orchestra of signs flash on
and off leaving Marilyn and all the other passengers
confused about whether they should start or stop
smoking amongst other things so Marilyn pretends not to
notice as things get a little crazy on board flight Q03 and
goes back to her list and the bit about Durrell.

*Then Durrell takes her hand and whispers in
her ear and when he stands up she follows
him and Lawrence follows her and they
all go and sit in a neat circle on Durrell's bed
and Durrell says thickly:*

*'I've got something you're really going to
love it's really great you just dip your
finger in I mean I promise you you've
never had anything like it.'*

So they all dip lick suck and pass and

29

*pretty soon they're all smiling and then
Lawrence leaves closing the door and then
Durrell says:*

'Follow me.'

*And the woman follows him into a
walk-in wardrobe where they sit down
under the neat row of suits and jackets
and the woman motormouth is talking:*

*'You see I was a boy I mean a boyish girl
and no-one liked me and I hated school
because I was in love with this guy that
everyone was in love with and I was so
glad to leave school because this guy just
never rang back and he didn't like me but he
likes me now and I don't like him and
then I met hairy snail Lawrence and got
stoned for the first time and I love champagne don't you?'*

*Durrell dips licks sucks and passes
talking about all the desperate tortured
failed loves of his life and the way he can't
ever seem to meet anyone who's just nice
who doesn't expect everything all at once all
the time beyond his wildest dreams and
then the woman tells the story of how she
picked a guy up once at a party by saying:*

*'Give me your phone number and then
you can give me a call,' which she thought
was pretty funny at the time and soon the
conversation begins to drift around words
and occasionally the woman comes up
with a good word like:*

'Facetious.'

30

And Durrell laughs and the woman starts to laugh and then Durrell says thickly:

'What?'

And then the woman says:

'What do you mean "what"?'

And then Durrell says:

'What was the word?'

And then the woman starts laughing which seems the best answer to the question until she stops and then she says:

'I can't remember what I was laughing at.'

And then Durrell says:

'I think you were laughing about forgetting.'

And so on until the woman says:

'Facetious.'

And Durrell says:

'That's the word.'

And the woman says:

'What does it mean?'

And:

'Who would have thought up such a word?'

And:

'It's a great word.'

And then Durrell says:

'I saw this really funny movie the other day called something about Tin the Tin oh God I can't remember the name anyway it had that actor in it you know the really short guy fat and really funny you know* *don't you? What's his name?'*

And the woman says:

'What was the question?'

And Durrell says:

'Well anyway there's this scene where he smashes into this car and they've got two Cadillacs these two guys and one of them's brand new and the other guy's driving along and they crash and it's really funny you know? I was laughing so much I thought I was going to give myself a lobotomy and anyway what was I talking about? Oh yeah.'

And then Durrell just keeps talking and the woman realises quite calmly and happily that something is going to happen between herself and this smudgy blue-eyed motormouth boy and suddenly feels full of the sort of wholesome sunny Sunday morning joyfulness that's a little bit like all the goodness emanating from a nicely arranged fruit bowl and she's almost bursting with buoyancy as she reaches over and in a very schoolgirl-hockey-team way puts her arm around his shoulders and gives him a friendly squeeze knowing the expression on her face probably unfortunately resembles the face of an indulged baby golden retriever that she thinks a friend of hers probably owned at some stage or another.

Meanwhile Durrell vaguely senses that there is a woman in his walk-in wardrobe

32

smiling at him in this indulged-baby-
golden-retriever way with her arm around
his shoulders giving him jovial squeezes
that strike him as being very schoolgirl-
hockey-team and he begins to suspect that
something must have happened but isn't
really sure what and it's only in the
process of reaching for his book of John
Laws' poetry that is absolutely indispensable
in these sorts of situations that he becomes
uncomfortably aware of his male urges in
terms of a very real and solid physical
presence and in a flash he remembers the
shared seconds of frozen time in the seemingly fresh spring rain that stood still tangible as a raindrop when they'd all seemed to
know what was going to happen and as he
carefully opens the ragged hardback
edition to his favourite poem his eyes
become smudgily stuck to her face and a
super-size smile settles spread-eagled all
over everything and he starts talking
about what a nice girl she is and how he's
always found her devastatingly attractive
and then he sort of loses the point of what
he's saying because her name eludes him
so he points at the poem with his stumpy
little finger and the woman takes his
finger with their eyes still stuck together
and eventually places it within the dry
sticky cavity of her mouth and then
Durrell puts some drugs onto another
finger so that the woman has two fingers in

the dry sticky cavity of her mouth and
incapable of sucking in a vacuum she
manages to simulate sucking by gulping
dryly and profusely but eventually finds
this too exhausting and stops and they sit
there for a while his fingers in her mouth
their eyes stuck together smiling panting
and gasping for air.

And at some point Durrell forgets what
he's doing and his eyes come unstuck and
slowly slide down her face along her neck
and down the black linen dress to the little
plastic packet on her lap and he suddenly
smiles and as he reaches for the packet
tearing inches of skin from the inside of
her mouth and little flakes from her lips
he says:

'This is very nice isn't it?'

And then they share the last few dips
and the woman takes hold of his hand
and massages it authoritatively cracking
all the knuckles precisely and individually
holding onto hovering thoughts and drifting
passions and revelations keep surfacing
and disappearing mysteriously before they
can be put into words or even finished
and after a while the conversation
emerges again from the murky deep when
the woman says something about it being a
fantastic party with the best people and
food and drinks and music she's been to
in a long time and it's just at that moment
that the fireworks begin to go off in

*regular booms and faint flashes of colour
creep in and form patterns on the floor
and then Durrell kisses the woman and
says:*

'Happy New Year.'

*And then he kisses her again and
although at first she thinks she's going to die
because she can't breathe the woman finds
herself concentrating on the idea of kissing in
a vacuum and then she thinks:*

Vacuum's a great word.

And then she wonders:

What was the vacuum?

And:

Where?

*And it's not long before Durrell
undresses her and then they lie naked
under all the hanging clothes as the fireworks boom away and then Durrell
makes love to her slowly and deeply predictable as a piston and the woman realises her whole face aches from smiling and
that her teeth are numb and that she needs a
glass of water and Durrell seems to take
forever but after he's sated his male urges she
is sorry because as soon as he stops she
wants him to keep going so she mumbles
words to that effect and Durrell hugs and
kisses her and says:*

'OK.'

*But they just lie there like two beached
salamanders   sweating   smiling   and
gasping.*

And all of a sudden the captain's voice booms into the middle of the action and the sleeping man sits bolt upright and says:

'Was I asleep? Was I snoring? Did my snoring keep you awake?'

And Marilyn nods yes and shakes no twice and within seconds they're only inches above the runway at Honolulu airport so Marilyn carefully closes the notebook and places the logoed biro back on the doily'd dish and just as the plane touches down she looks up to meet the gaze of the lousy hack air hostess who smiles and then looks away and Marilyn secretly hopes that they change cabin crew in Honolulu because she's beginning to feel the persistent nagging gurglings of an empty slushy wine soaked digestive tract.

and:
Honolulu Honolulu.

Honolulu is just one long neon dream on a moving footway in a long white tunnel and if that was the horror of the US customs experience then it wasn't nearly as unpleasant or scandalous or horrendous as Marilyn had been led to believe and it isn't until she's back on the plane that she realises she hasn't noticed much about Honolulu at all because the only thought she can drag out and hold onto has something to do with a face and a TV screen and a certain sense of desolate windswept inevitability and:

Oh Twentiethcentury.

And butterflies and Christmas beetles rush to her stomach and haunted crispy cicada shells start tap dancing down her small intestine and it's only when Marilyn is finally on the verge of internal-haemorrhaging that she manages to mouth the words that let everyone on flight Q03 know that she's more than a little hungry:

'Where the fuck's my dinner?'

And as the buzzing whizzing of a migraine makes itself at home beneath her sweaty scalp and her eyes gracefully roll back in her head and her eyelids flutteringly close over the whites Bette the lousy hack air hostess sits down in the next seat bearing

a certain sense

of desolate

windswept

inevitability

37

gifts of medicines and cool salves and pungent scents with a knit brow that's half plain half pearl still wondering about the notebook and the woman and Lawrence.

But Marilyn doesn't notice when Bette sits down in the seat that's been recently vacated by the sleeping man in the row of popular emergency exit seats because she's surrendered to delirious delicious daydreams and is lost in a remembrance of things past that starts with a phone call from Virginia on New Year's Day.

And Virginia says:

'Hi Marilyn this is Virginia you know from Durrell's party? remember we talked about going to New York together?'

And Marilyn answers cautiously in the affirmative and then Virginia's voice babbles on from beneath her beaky nose in her long lined face:

'You know Marilyn I know all about what's been going on between you and Lawrence and I just wanted to tell you that I've been through a really similar experience myself and I think we should get together this afternoon for a drink to compare notes and talk homegrown psychiatry and psychology and about learning to recognise deep-seated needs and desires cheaply and effectively.'

And a few hours later Marilyn and Virginia meet in a bar and talk home-grown psychiatry and psychology and compare notes and become intoxicated asphyxiated and inebriated and that's when they invent a world of their own which is:

'. . . a pool . . .'

'. . . a swirling pool . . .'

'. . . of tropical fruits . . .'

'. . . and macadamia nuts . . .'
'. . . and gin . . .'
And giggles.
'. . . and lots of blow-up pink elephants . . .'
'. . . giving foot massages . . .'
'. . . and acupuncture . . .'
And more giggles.
And Marilyn laughs to herself and Bette thinks:
She's just another crazy dumb fuck broad.

Meanwhile Marilyn's delirious delicious daydreams take flight and wave magic wands and fly away suddenly frightened by the lingering presence of a few of life's nastier looming questions and Marilyn starts to worry about black holes and gaps and mumbles:

'But how did Virginia know about what's been happening between Lawrence and me?'

Which is a very nasty looming question and closely followed by another:

'Does that mean Virginia knows all about Durrell and Miller as well?'

And another:

'Is Virginia psychic? or a closet astrologist? or some kind of psychopathic home-breaker?'

But the nastiest question:

'Has Virginia told Lawrence about Durrell and Miller?' looms last.

And this is why Marilyn's oblivious to Bette who as a direct result of secretly reading Marilyn's notebook is coming to terms with the knowledge that she's led a very boring and sheltered existence for a glamorous air hostess who's really a budding actress and while Marilyn wonders about gaps and black holes Bette says:

'I just can't believe it's taken me this long to realise that up until now I've only ever scratched the crackly dry surface of interpersonal communication.'

And this possibility shakes the firey molten rock core of her very being.

So it's with trembling butterfly hands and wild staring eyes and flaring nostrils that Bette pours herself a glass of wine and closes her eyes and lets her thoughts slip and slide and her nostrils deflate and pretty soon she realises that Marilyn is mumbling and this is what she thinks Marilyn is saying:

'I'm searching for the answers to life's looming questions.'

And Bette says:

'Me too.'

Then Marilyn says:

'Life is a matter of who's sleeping with who and who knows and who doesn't know.'

And Bette wonders:

Is it?

And then Marilyn says:

'So we bought a bottle of gin and went back to Virginia's flat.'

And Bette thinks:

Who's Virginia?

And that's when Marilyn goes into a rave about Virginia:

'And during the course of the conversation we spontaneously and simultaneously click and at some stage Virginia decides to spend her entire inheritance on travelling the world and says that she'd like to take me as well and we decide to go to New York first because of Bronte and then we polish off a magnum of wine and then

I pass out and the next thing I know Virginia's saying:

'"I'm bleeding I'm bleeding."

'And I say:

'"Shut up and go back to sleep we'll talk about it in the morning," thinking she's talking about her period or something but that's before I open my sealed-in-gin red bleary eyes and see the standing knife dripping blood from Virginia's wrists which means that she doesn't have her period but that she's probably just tried to kill herself and my arms are too heavy to do anything and I'm altogether too drunk and tired to really care and even though the blood just keeps on dripping—

'*Drip drip drip*—

'I just grab the standing knife and put it under my pillow and go back to sleep.

'And then the next morning I find Virginia's deeply enigmatic note which says:

'*Dear Marilyn gone to a friend's house.*

'And after that there's a long smear of blood and then it says:

'*I'll meet you at the airport near gate 12 at 12 p.m. OK? Pack light Virginia.*

'And then there's more blood and then I collapse in a heap.'

Meanwhile, Lawrence and Durrell and Miller and Virginia have all begun to dance eerily up and down the aisles of Bette's mind and she's just about to tap Marilyn on the shoulder and tell her all about her lifelong dream of becoming an actress and moving to Hollywood when all of a sudden Marilyn opens her eyes and in a series of wild gestures she takes up her pen and notebook and indifferent to Bette's hypnotic stare and gently prodding fingers writes:

Several hours later the woman is staring out her window at her view of Sydney Harbour unable to remember a lot of seemingly important events like:

How did I get home from Virginia's house?

And:

How did I meet Virginia in the first place?

And the last thing she can remember is waking up under a pile of clothes and coathangers suffering from retinal burnout at Durrell's house and it's only after she rereads the note from Virginia that she finds in her pocket that she begins to remember some of the things she's forgotten like:

Getting drunk.

And:

Going to New York with the money from Virginia's inheritance.

So she closes the blinds and takes off her clothes and lies down on the day after New Year's Day and then the woman dreams:

I'm swinging in a swing in Central Park kicking up the dead leaves with my bare feet and staring up through the bare branches of the dead trees at a typical wintry sky when an elephant with a human head with something nonsensical written across its forehead tries to mug me and I try to run away but I can't because it's a dream and before I can wake up to stop the elephant mugging me I see an ice-skating rink and race out onto the ice and even though I'm not wearing any skates I can still glide along on my bare feet which are suddenly as smooth as glass and as I skate I sort of flap my arms like wings because somehow it's just like flying.

And the elephant tries to follow me out onto the ice but slips and I watch as the ice cracks and then a yellow road suddenly opens up in the ice and I skate up the yellow road and over a bridge just like in The Wizard of Oz *and then skate down the other side and on through Manhattan flapping until I take off.*

And then I'm flying like a stork in a cartoon which is nothing like gliding but more like bobbing up and down with each flap just managing to get over all the skyscrapers and it doesn't take long before I'm too tired to go on and then all of a sudden I'm falling and I'm just about to crash into a bus and I think:

I'm not really flying I'm ice-skating.

And I start moving my feet but nothing happens and I fall.

Bette interprets the dream for Marilyn and decides that the elephant symbolises all the men in her life but then Bette gets caught up in the words as Marilyn's pen continues to dance across the page and then Bette reads all about Twentiethcentury Fox's historic television appearance:

> *The woman wakes up covered in sweat with her intestines tied up in fisherman's knots and whole marching armies of butterflies and Christmas beetles let her know that she's more than a little hungry.*
>
> *And she's so unnerved and traumatised by the dream that she switches on the TV for company as she rushes through the lounge room to the kitchen where she fixes herself a toasted sandwich which she hungrily wolfs down and because she's in the middle of a manic desperation depression she makes another one and wolfs that down too and she's somewhere in the middle of making the third toasted sandwich when Twentiethcentury Fox makes one of his historic television appearances and the woman stops making the toasted sandwich and is instantly mesmerised by that no-I-never-did-have-my-adenoids-out-so-yes-I-do-have-a-sinus-condition accent and despite her allergy and all the unwelcome side effects she is magnetically and inevitably drawn into the lounge room and that's when she first notices Twentiethcentury Fox's beneath-the-appearance dishevelled self and the jaded world-weary look about his face as tears stream down her cheeks and is intrigued and fascinated between sneezes by everything he's saying because she*

knows he's talking about money although she doesn't understand a thing because it's all very abstract and about seats which don't mean much to her.

And it seems to the woman that his suit is like a chrysalis that he could burst out of at any second and then crawl out like a little pink larva and finally fly away in a yellow blue and black cloud and she doesn't notice his brown eyes or brown hair or the colour of the stripes in his tie or the shape of his hands or any of the details of his impeccable does-he-really-work-in-Wall-Street? business suit or any of the things you're supposed to notice about a person when you first meet them and they make an impact on you that's something like a swift hard smack across the face.

The woman gently touches her left cheek as if she's just been smacked in the face and it feels hot and tingly and wet and she sits down and tries to stop sneezing and nurses her raw red rubbed nose and tastes a dry blood taste in the back of her throat and wonders what it all means.

And she notices between sniffles that the host of the talk show is interested and impressed by everything Twentiethcentury Fox is saying although the woman doesn't understand how you can make all that money from nothing or the way money seems to be able to appear out of nothing at all.

> *And then during the interview his name*
> *flashes up onto the screen and the woman*
> *writes it down on a piece of newspaper and*
> *folds it and puts it on the table and when the*
> *commercials come on she switches off the*
> *TV and sits staring stunned and brainless at*
> *the screen and as she wolfs down the third*
> *toasted sandwich it occurs to her that it*
> *might be a good idea to ring Twentieth-*
> *century Fox because she realises she has to*
> *meet him because he's the first person she's*
> *ever met who she's wanted to tell her whole*
> *life story to and more.*

And Bette thinks:

You're the first person I've ever met who I've
wanted to tell my whole life story to and more.

Meanwhile Marilyn lays down the logoed biro and
sighs and all of a sudden it's just as if they've both been
drained of all their precious bodily fluids and thinly
sliced and then spread out like two slices of carpaccio
waiting to be dressed in lemon and olive oil and gar-
nished with freshly ground black pepper and a sprig of
parsley.

And that's when—

Wow—

Marilyn empathetically opens her hand to receive
the little package of white powdered drugs just as Bette
passes it to her and then Marilyn smiles thanks and
heads off to a toilet cubicle staggering along the aisle all
soon-to-be-sated anticipation and glee.

as soon as Marilyn leaves Bette finds herself alone at last with Marilyn's purchased-just-prior-to-departure now-I'm-going-to-keep-a-travel-diary notebook as it lies unguarded and naked on top of her fold-up tray and Bette seizes the empathetic moment to read some more of *The List of Names and Places*.

But Bette only makes it halfway through the bit about Durrell's party when she casts a guilty glance down the aisle and—

Oh no—

Here comes Marilyn in leaps and bounds so she sneaks the spiral notebook back onto the tray and thinks:

That's really amazing.

But what Bette really means when she thinks this is that she thinks Marilyn's *The List of Names and Places* has launched an unsuspecting humanity and anybody else who happens to be around at the time smack bang into the middle of an exciting exploration down a little-known avenue of the human condition.

Although Bette doesn't say anything to Marilyn about this and after they've both been sitting uncomfortably in their emergency exit seats for a few minutes wanting to tuck their legs up or stretch their legs out and get horizontal or stick their heads out windows for a breath of fresh air they share a second empathetic communication and they simultaneously think:

I really want to talk to you and tell you my life story and float ideas between us while everyone else is watching the Hollywood movie on video and I've seen it at the movies anyway.

And then Marilyn says to Bette:

toothsome things

'So you see then I ring Twentiethcentury Fox and this woman called Liz answers the phone and I think she's Twentiethcentury's housekeeper and when she says he isn't there I just keep ringing her back because I know I have to talk to Twentiethcentury and then I think well maybe she's Twentiethcentury's wife and so she doesn't want to give him my messages because of what might happen if she does and that's when I realise I have to see him and so I think of Virginia's offer and I remember I have to meet her at twelve so I write down Twentiethcentury's address and start packing and grab a couple of hundred dollars and get ready to leave.'

Just then Bette feels an overwhelming need to speak despite all her shyness and reluctance to open up to anyone let alone a complete stranger so she leans forward in her seat and starts to gesture with her hands and to lick her lips profusely and her nostrils flare and her eyes stare wildly and even though her hair is clinging to the chair because of physics and static electricity she still manages to say:

'You're the first person I've ever met who I've really wanted to tell my entire life story to and I feel like I've known you for years even though we've only just met and by the way my name's Bette.'

And Marilyn becomes vaguely aware that Bette's whirring words and flaring nostrils and wild staring eyes and widely smiling mouth and shaking out-stretched hand all expect some kind of response so Marilyn nods and is just about to say something about Lawrence when Bette says:

'And i guess that's why my life up until now has been little more than a blind pilgrimage with no Mecca not really wanting to talk to anyone before do you know what I mean?'

But Marilyn isn't really listening and interrupts:

'You see I had the affairs with Miller and Durrell because I was so confused about Lawrence because he kept making fun of my allergies but now suddenly everything's so clear since Twentiethcentury and from the moment I first saw him on that TV matinee show and he first made me sneeze it was like we were two people staring at each other from different sides of a windswept street in a chilly desolate wintry cityscape.'

Which makes Bette even more determined to speak in spite of Marilyn's motormouth and the few strands of hair clinging to the corners of her mouth:

'That's just how I feel because suddenly everything's really clear for me too and life's just like that it's just like two people staring at each other all chilly and desolate and I just can't believe that it's taken me this long to realise that life's really so simple.'

And Marilyn's still talking:

'I'm just not completely sure about how I'm going to deal with Liz.'

And then Bette pauses to remove some of the soggy strands of hair and says:

'You know what it's like? Can I tell you what life's like?'

But Marilyn's deeply lost in schemes of trickery and deceit and doesn't hear Bette say:

'Hollywood life's just like Hollywood you know you've just got to get in there with everyone else and claw your way to the top yeah that's what life is that's the meaning of life.'

And that's when Marilyn says:

'Shit,' because just at that moment Marilyn and Bette are both almost thrown out of their popular emergency exit seats as the plane begins its wobbly sorry-about-the-air-pockets-folks descent which makes Bette leap up in a panic to strap Marilyn back in her seat and tilt her chair upright and fold away her tray and clear away the empty bottles and cups and doily'd dishes and then she mesmerises Marilyn with a long I'm-really-glad-I-met-you stare and then whispers a quick conspiratorial confession in Marilyn's ear:

'Life may be just like Hollywood but it's nothing like the sort of bullshit I went through during my extremely unhappy repressive childhood which was made even more unbearable by incest and that's when I decided to become an air hostess to escape and now I understand why all that happened to me and no-one will be able to say:

'"Oh she's just really screwed up," about me any more when I pass out in corners at parties because I've discovered the importance of Hollywood and the meaning of life.'

And suddenly the wheels touch down and Bette remembers about being an air hostess and drifts up the aisle like a lousy hack rearranging her uniform and smoothing down her hair.

Marilyn closes her eyes because Bette's conspiratorial confession about Hollywood and the meaning of life and incest makes her head spin and some of life's nastier looming questions begin to creep around the dark patches of her mind and as her tongue begins to whirl involuntarily around her lips smearing the remains of her expensive Grace Kelly lipstick in ever widening whirligig circles she indulges in a pre-disembarkation fantasy that's all about Virginia and Lawrence and lime pickles and is her imaginary answer to some of life's nastier looming questions:

The Imaginary Lime Pickle Incident

An incredibly attractive man who has eyes like a possum and who's a bit of a hairy snail finishes his mountain of walnut and chocolate cake and double clotted King Island cream with gusto and savours the last scoop with noisy smacking lips and then licks the plate to a highly polished sheen and places it carefully back on the smooth laminex table.

Looking up he meets the steady stare of two beady eyes that belong to a woman with a long lined face and a creased baggy linen suit sitting at another table in the busy bistro and when the waiter places a browned bulging strawberry soufflé on a giant white plate in front of the woman she raises her eyebrows at the incredibly attractive man who winks and cocks his finger like a gun before pushing back his chair with a screech and swaggering over to her table just like a B-grade actor playing a flawed hero in a low-budget third-rate Hollywood Disaster Movie and the waiter brings another spoon so they share the browned bulging strawberry soufflé slowly and silently.

And when they've both finished they lay down their spoons and whimper contentment and lean back in their chairs and take small sips of water and then they start talking about homemade ice-cream and papaya from Singapore and fresh lychees and figs and juicy white peaches and crisp delicious apples in Paris from Tasmania and then they chat about homemade pasta especially cannelloni and then they move onto other

51

*noodles which leads them into Thai food and how to pre-
serve chillies which ultimately leads into the specifics
of condiments which is where they reach the point of lime
pickles and the incredibly attractive man leans close to the
woman with the long lined face and gazes deeply into her
beady eyes and says:*

*'Back at my place I have some lime pickles that
were made from limes grown in our family orchard
which I'd really like you to try.'*

*And on the way back to the incredibly attractive
man's house the woman with the long lined face and
creased baggy linen suit says:*

*'I'm taking Marilyn to New York tomorrow
because she needs a break from Sydney and all the
affairs she's been having with other men and she's very
confused about you because of the way you tease her in
front of people at dinner parties about her allergies but I
can understand that you mightn't want to talk about it
right now.'*

And the incredibly attractive man nods:

*'You're right I don't want to talk about it right
now.'*

*And the first thing the woman with the beady eyes
notices about his flat is the smell of lemon blossoms
and damp towels which reminds her of old books like the
ones in her mother's leadlight bookcases at home and
meanwhile the man who's a bit of a hairy snail disappears
into the kitchen to hunt for his stash of lime pickles so she
opens the French doors onto a little wrought-iron
balcony where the air blows around crisp and cool and
where she gazes up at the haunted werewolf moon and
watches the high fast-flowing clouds flurry past and
she huddles a little in her baggy linen jacket as the*

wind blows her hair around her face and waits and she smiles when the incredibly attractive man produces a shiny glass jar and a little silver spoon and a bottle of red wine and some water biscuits and cheese talking about how he wants to be a photographer so he can take pictures of naked women with all sorts of food and then he asks if she's hungry and if she feels like ordering out for sashimi or a fruit platter or other toothsome things.

And Marilyn remembers with a sigh how meeting Lawrence was just like a breath of fresh air under a wide sky full of stars on a crystal clear winter night out in the country as the fog rolls in and how they'd stayed awake all night out on the balcony eating and talking about toothsome things and then she thinks about saying goodbye at the airport maybe forever and a cold pang of something nasty shoots through her system as she imagines Virginia savouring deep breaths of lemon blossoms and damp towels.

And this is why Marilyn doesn't look out the window and notice Manhattan the beast with its thousand invisible eyes and twin bronze brontosaurus heads peering shortsighted into the steamy fog and smiling hello at her as it crouches patiently at the edge of the water guarding the grey expanse where the two mighty rivers meet with the grey towers of Midtown lurking hungry in the background like older relatives.

and when Marilyn disembarks all jelly-legged confusion she's not sure whether the fantasy about Lawrence and Virginia and lime pickles is real or imaginary and she's still wondering whether Lawrence and Virginia are together as she waves goodbye to her emergency exit seat although this jelly-legged confusion is only a passing thing and it's not long before the horror of the US customs experience shatters the hallucinatory quality of flight Q03 into a million trillion tiny pieces and Marilyn realises with an almost hysterical acceleration of her tired and feverish senses that she's within an hour of her final destination and her immediate goal in life so she hurries outside towards the taxi rank with her bags in tow.

Her first gasp of icy cold makes her cough and splutter dizzily and while she's waiting in the queue she watches the way her breath comes out in steaming jets before hanging around her face and getting drippy and as she glances from one well-fed impeccably well-dressed businessman's face to another she thinks:

Surely they can't all work on Wall Street?

And suddenly Lawrence and Durrell and Miller and Virginia and everything else in Sydney seem far far away like faint faded fancies from another distant

an almost

hysterical

acceleration of

her tired and

feverish senses

once-upon-a-time place and Marilyn realises that up until now her entire life has been little more than a series of detours down deserted side streets waiting for meteors to drop or stars to fall and then she feels a powerful rush of energy surging through the white water rivers of her central nervous system and the crispy cicada shells and haunted Christmas beetles that live in her stomach begin spinning on their backs and Marilyn no longer feels like she's mindlessly watching her life pass by before her on a TV screen whose picture is so infested with white noise that the action is almost imperceptible and all generational analyses of the information are well and truly out of the question because she suddenly feels like she's passed inside something because everything's so much more in focus and brighter and much more present and immediate and it's like she's suddenly been instantaneously transformed into a famous rap-star—

Yo!

And in her mind's eye she's just about to do a mostly-live performance on an all-night video show when a large black man wearing a gold ring through his nose propels her from the cab rank on the cheerless chilly footpath into the back seat of a battered yellow cab and soon the powerful rush of energy begins to subside and her thoughts begin to slip soporific and she drifts into a delicious delirious daydream that resembles an expensive made-for-commercial-TV advertisement and she dreams about a large brass bed with lots of fluffy feather pillows and a giant-sized goose down quilt and all the bed linen is crisp and cotton and white and a little bit scratchy from drying outside in all the fresh sunny air on a clothesline and the bed has four wooden bedposts with delicate white lace draping all the way down to the floor and it's not long before Marilyn's entire body begins to ache and tremble at the idea of horizontal perception.

Meanwhile Twentiethcentury Solomon Fox coaxes his body towards his first bowel movement of the day with a bowl of toasted-in-prune-juice-and-honey hi-fibre bran which is happily swimming free-style in a brownish puddle of soya milk and pretends to flick through the memos left by his secretary on his large desk and looks out over the Hudson River to New Jersey.

On the day Marilyn arrives the water is a choppy steely greeny grey beneath cloudy skies and looks just like it looked yesterday and the day before and the day before that and on and on and so on and Twentiethcentury says:

'Fucken rip off,' and grunts gruffly to himself as his thoughts begin their inevitable daily descent into the deep nebulous caverns of sensation where memory flickers and drips in damp limestone caves of recollection and this is where Twentiethcentury comes every morning to paint the sweeping sunsets and frosty dawns of his childhood Upstate all over today and yesterday and tomorrow and sometimes the beginnings of a poem or a song will bloom all apple blossoms in the spring and he hums the first few lines of yesterday's Downtown traffic jam song:

> *Choking on exhaust fumes*
> *reeling while your head booms*
> *listen to the old tunes*
>
> *Rattling round your head*

But that's where he keeps getting stuck because he can't think of anything to rhyme with head other than dead but then suddenly these blurry hazy pleasantries give way soft as peat to the razor-sharp edge of obsession as Twentiethcentury farts loudly and says:

'Excuse me,' and blushes pale pink and pushes his breakfast to one side and then pads through luscious pile to his private en suite where he spreads his plump rump over the padded seat and makes weary calculations of information flows and internal audits and tries desperately and unsuccessfully to forget all about the recent landslide in the profitability of his current emotional prospect Garbo and the resulting unfulfilling slump in the productivity of their relationship.

While Twentiethcentury Fox agonises between information flows and slumps in profitability in his relationship with Garbo Marilyn wearily closes her eyes and lies down on the gargantuan vinyl seat and she doesn't notice that it smells like cigarettes and beer and fish and chips in vinegar and stale sweat and dry blood or look out the window at the long stretch of Flatbush Avenue or the bare trees against the wintry sky or the banked up early morning where-are-all-these-cars-going? traffic because she slips soporific into a dream:

I'm standing at the end of a queue for a movie and the queue seems to stretch ahead of me for miles and miles across streets and past the gloomy tiles of subway stations and around corners and I think:

I'm never going to get to the end of the queue and even if I do all the seats will be sold out by the time I get there anyway and maybe I should just run and push to the front.

And my breath begins to come in quick shallow gasps and my knees turn to jelly and I'm just about to make a run for it when I realise my legs won't move and seem to be stuck to the spot and a sort of meltdown occurs on the street and everything bloats and wobbles and then everything shrinks and shrivels and that's when I divine the dulcet tones of that no-I-never-did-have-my-adenoids-out-so-yes-I-do-have-a-sinus-condition accent gruffly grunting somewhere further down the queue and I crane my head to see and begin to sweat and my pulse races because the voice sounds strangely familiar as it says:

'I mean like listen to this I mean this is exactly what I'm talking about I mean will you listen to this guy going on about Marshall McLuhan as if he knows him? I mean he's really beginning to annoy me like he's spraying the back of my neck with spit I mean this guy's one hell of a king-size pain in the ass.'

And I'm just standing there listening because my legs won't move but I can't stand still either because I have to find out who it is and then suddenly I turn around and Twentiethcentury Fox is standing right behind me in the queue and as I look deeply into his eyes for the second time it's just like we're two people staring at each other from different sides of a windswept street in a chilly desolate wintry cityscape and he turns and walks away and I follow him out onto the street and suddenly I look up and there's a car coming straight at me and I try to scream but nothing comes out and I can't move and the car gets closer and closer and then we're sitting on a park bench in the sun in

Central Park watching as the people go gliding by on ice skates and we're laughing and Twentiethcentury squeezes my shoulder and birds are singing in the bare trees and when Twentiethcentury turns around to kiss me I see that he's not Twentiethcentury at all and that he's someone else and as the face oozes and bloats and shrinks and pulsates I realise he's Woody Allen and then I start laughing and I can't stop.

And Marilyn wakes up laughing and tastes the nasty God-I-feel-like-a-piece-of-shit taste in her mouth that follows any significant air travel experience and she opens her eyes just in time to see an enormous billboard with—

COCAINE—

Written across it in large bold black letters as big as a house on a peeling white background and that's when she finally notices that the gargantuan vinyl seat smells like cigarettes and beer and fish and chips and vinegar and stale sweat and dry blood and Marilyn looks out the window at the long stretch of Flatbush Avenue and the bare trees against the grey wintry sky and the bleakly stained dingy drab apartment blocks and the banked up where-are-all-these-cars-going? traffic and her eyes are dry and rubbery and her scalp itches and prickles and Marilyn wonders:

Am I dead yet?

And then closes her eyes again and sinks back into a drowsy daze where Twentiethcentury Fox is sitting on a deckchair on his private yacht somewhere off the coast of Maine wearing red braces and a white shirt and doing business by phone sipping Perrier which reminds her that she's almost reached her final destination and she hopes Twentiethcentury isn't home so she has a chance to freshen up before she meets him face to face and with considerable oh-my-God-where-are-the-toothpicks-for-my-eyes? concentration she struggles back to a sitting position and simulates chirpy alertness as the cab edges into the tunnel to Manhattan.

Meanwhile Liz sits shivering on her hard bench behind her bookstall at Central Park and watches herself in the shop window across the road between passing traffic as the sun bounces off her shiny curls and checks the angle of her hat and that it goes with her scarf overcoat and sunglasses and decides that the yellow sunglasses make her skin seem yellow against the emerald green scarf and just as she takes them off to polish them with a kleenex a large black stretch limo cruises close by like a hungry shark and stops at a red light.

And Twentiethcentury looks out behind tinted windows at the young girl sitting at the bookstall in the sun with dark luscious curls and an emerald green scarf polishing her sunglasses and imagines a simple carefree life in a tiny loft with a thumping gurgling central heating system and a futon bed and not much else and just the two of them living on tins of beans through the winter reading books and writing poetry only leaving their warm cosy bed to visit the cafe on the corner where they listen to the band and sip Irish coffees and then the girl puts on her sunglasses and Twentiethcentury curses his haemorrhoids and sighs an angry grunting sigh because this morning's shit was one of those ones that disappear straight up the back which bodes evil for the day's business proceedings and

Twentiethcentury curses the servants of Satan who long ago seized control of his intestines—

Fucken rip off—

And returns to his contemplation of the lunch menu with its predictable proliferation of all things cooked in salt sugar and fat and grunts gruffly and says to his driver:

'How do they get away with dishing out this crap day in day out I mean like what's wrong with a little home-made coleslaw with reduced-cholesterol oil or some steamed vegetables with sesame seeds or some tofu or something like that?'

And the driver sits silent recognising the no-response-required rhetoric of today's seemingly constipated consistently flatulent customer.

And Twentiethcentury looks out the window again just in time to see a horse drop a steaming pile of turd on the cobblestones and feels his chest tighten as his testes shrivel and his anus contracts and as he shifts his plump rump to one side in stifled outrage the horse seems to fix him malignantly with a single wild blinkered eye before swishing its tail and trotting off into the traffic with its buggy full of Japanese tourists in loud fits of giggles.

And Liz almost gags on the fresh earthy stench as her breakfast of French fries and egg nog threatens to come loose from her stomach and she turns to face the direction of the wind and stores her disgust away for a rainy day when she makes her lucky break in an Off Off Broadway play and prays a silent prayer that her flatmates will have some good ideas about paying next month's rent when she arrives home shivering blue and chapped with another book she knows she'll never read.

*

Meanwhile Marilyn struggles in a dark death-like daze convinced that she has been swallowed whole by some large beast with a thousand invisible eyes and twin brontosaurus heads and that right this second she is plummeting down its greasy gullet like last week's gorgonzola to its festering fungi filled gizzard where she'll be ground in gastric juices before disappearing into a putrid pit of primordial green slime never to see Twentiethcentury ever again and she begins to panic and calls out for help and the driver looks in the mirror and says:

'You must be Ostralian,' as the cab edges back into the icy grey light.

While far far away in another distant once-upon-a-time place Miller is sitting on his batik bed couch wondering about Marilyn and why she never answers the phone and who's collecting her mail and whether she's dead or alive because he still can't get her out of his mind and even though his wife's back he wants to see Marilyn again just one more time so they can do all the things people do when they've lusted after each other for a long time again and maybe this time he'll be able to tell her all about his deepest desires although he begins to suspect that he's seen the last of Marilyn and her very liberal yes-I'm-yours attitude and he mumbles something to his wife about buying the papers and leaves to try to ring Marilyn from the public phone on the corner and feels foolish and empty when he hangs up the phone.

Meanwhile Twentiethcentury sits at another red light and writes the next verse of yesterday's Downtown traffic jam song and imagines asking the driver to wait on the corner while he jogs the few blocks back to the girl with the dark shiny curls and the emerald green scarf and then he could show her the words of the song and hum a little of the tune and then maybe he'd ask her for her phone number and then she'd smile and shake her head and ask him for his instead and say she likes the song and then he'd smile and walk whistling back to the limo a little giddy from running.

> *Choking on exhaust fumes*
> *reeling while your head booms*
> *listen to the old tunes*
>
> *Rattling round your head*
> *Rattling round your head.*
>
> *Diet coke baked beans*
> *you and me our TV screen*
> *wonder what it all means*
>
> *Drag yourself out of bed*
> *Drag yourself out of bed.*

And Twentiethcentury eases his glottis open and belches softly and reads the lyrics out loud instead and then hums the tune to himself for a while and eventually leans forward and grunts gruffly in the driver's ear:

'Like how do you deal with this traffic every day? I mean like it drives me crazy and you're in it all day? Like I kind of write poetry and I find that really helps you know? Relaxes me otherwise I'd be crazy by now.'

And the driver recognises the minimal response

required to this now-I'm-going-to-talk-about-myself-for-a-while rhetoric and says:

'Oh really? You write poetry?' and edges the black limo through the traffic as Twentiethcentury's gruffly grunting words drone on and on in that no-I-never-did-have-my-adenoids-out-so-yes-I-do-have-a-sinus-condition accent.

As the traffic heading into Manhattan begins to ease and the knots of cars unwind and begin to pick up speed Marilyn's driver starts to play a frenzied lane-changing game and runs red lights and howls his horn and shakes his fist out the window and swears and growls in foreign tongues and grows reckless about potholes with years of experience to numb the jarring effects of poor suspension and lousy breaks and they're only blocks away from Marilyn's final destination and immediate goal in life although she doesn't realise this at the time when—

Crash bang boom—

They hit an unusually deep pothole and the front of the cab bounces down and Marilyn bounces forward and then it bounces up and Marilyn bounces up and then the back wheels bounce down and Marilyn bounces down and then they bounce up and Marilyn bounces up and bounces right out of her seat and her head hits the roof of the cab with a thud and then suddenly everything is black and spinning yellow red and white meteors and falling stars and Marilyn sinks down with a sigh into a humming place of less than no dreams.

Several hours later Marilyn locks herself in Liz's bathroom and slumps down on the toilet seat and lets her eyes wander aimlessly over the grimy tiles and peeling paint and down into the rust-stained bathtub and up to the inch-thick layers of black dust on the window sill and all along the spidery cracks in the glass and out into the dark whirling snow and back along the dried-out plaster to the sagging ragged hand towel limp and blackened with use and up again to savour the grey fuzz clinging to the top of the dangling naked light bulb and down again to the grimy tiles and finally come to rest in puzzled contemplation of the funny china protrusion and the strange phenomenon of the sink with no plug which is overflowing with living breathing organisms who are swimming breaststroke and doing handstands and waving from their seething green porcelain pool.

Marilyn smiles and says:

'Hi guys.'

And then mumbles through her hair:

'I just don't know how much more of this I can take.'

And that's when a high rasping voice says:

'Psssst hey Marilyn.'

But Marilyn tries to ignore the voice and buries her face in her hands and thinks:

It's sending me

the strange

phenomenon of

the sink with no

plug

crazy and I'm seeing things and hearing voices and—

Then the high rasping voice says a little louder:

'Have faith Marilyn everything's going to be just fine and dandy.'

And Marilyn looks into the seething green porcelain pool and watches the living breathing organisms swimming breaststroke and one of the little potato shapes waves its short pudgy hand and says in its high rasping voice:

'Hey Marilyn don't worry your troubles are all over 'cos the one and only Little Johnny Wayne Manhattan's most friendly enzyme is going to help you find whoever it is you're looking for.'

And Marilyn rubs her eyes and stands up and runs her hands through her hair.

Then Marilyn looks in the smeary cracked mirror and notices how frazzled dazed and post-concussed she looks and says:

'Well I've really fucked up this time I mean here I am having a nervous breakdown in this crazy city oh so far away from home and family and friends and I've already completely lost track of Virginia and God knows what's happened to Twentiethcentury Fox but wherever he lives he sure as hell doesn't live here and I feel like some kind of telecommunications refugee or victim of International Directory disturbance and any minute I'm going to blow my gasket and completely freak out because I've got an enormous aching egg on my head and I'm probably suffering from concussion and maybe I'll start brain haemorrhaging and collapse on the grimy tiles all dizzy and nauseous and no-one'll hear me as I moan and groan my way to permanent brain damage or a lonely painful death if I'm not already dead that is.'

And then she looks back into the seething green porcelain pool where Little Johnny Wayne Manhattan's most friendly enzyme floats on his back in the scum and says from his yellow starry-eyed face:

'I can help you find Twentiethcentury.'

And Marilyn says:

'Oh yeah?'

And then the potato shape swishes its tadpole tail and disappears into the seething green.

Marilyn looks back into the mirror and says:

'Any minute I'm going to rush out onto the street and throw myself under a passing car or better still under a subway train.'

And that's when she decides to do battle with the strange phenomenon of the sink with no plug so she can wash her face and freshen up so she leans her mouth close to the seething green and shouts so the organisms can hear:

'OK you guys this is a stick up.'

And cocks her fingers like two pistols and aims both barrels into the seething green just like a B-grade actress playing a flawed heroine in a low-budget third-rate Hollywood Disaster Movie and says:

'Nobody move.'

And when nobody does and everything is still and quiet Marilyn holds her breath and closes her eyes and clamps her mouth tightly shut and then slowly lowers her hands into the gurgling durge through layers of warm scum and explores the stagnant waters with reluctant fingertips and no there isn't a plug and it's not long before she runs out of breath and is forced to admit defeat and executes a neat withdrawal cautious of speed and aqua dynamics and the sinister possibility of the bends and the unspoken threat of the decompression chamber and she holds her oozing hands to drip over the seething green porcelain pool.

Marilyn looks in the smeary cracked mirror between strands of hair and says:

'I mean I just can't believe Liz's as innocent of all this as she seems.'

And then resumes her attack with fresh tactics and as she gently explores the contours of the funny china protrusion she mumbles:

'I mean one minute she's taking messages as if Twentiethcentury lives here and then the next minute her flatmate's shrugging her shoulders and telling me that Twentiethcentury might turn up and that I should ask Liz when she gets home because she thinks her sister might have gone out with someone called Twentiethcentury.'

When suddenly—

Eeeeeech—

And the funny china protrusion surrenders its secret with an open sesame sigh and the seething green porcelain pool disappears down the hissing gurgling drain and the living breathing organisms take their last gasps of air and say their famous last words before they're swallowed with a savage sucking sound down the gloating greedy plug hole.

Marilyn smiles and straightens her shoulders triumphantly and decides to confront Liz about Twentiethcentury as soon as she comes home and Marilyn sprinkles the no-longer-phenomenal sink with no plug with generous dollops of generic non-brand powder cleanser and begins to scrub and rub until everything glistens and shines.

Finally Marilyn's hands grow still and she closes her eyes and indulges in a little remembrance of things past and this remembrance starts when she's lying unconscious in the back of a cab from JFK to Manhattan:

I'm floating on puffed-rice pockets of air and drifting in sweetly scented eddies and spirals and then I'm sinking down and drowning in a puddle of beer and stubbed out cigarette butts and deep-fried fish and chips and vinegar and something keeps brushing against my face which smells like stale sweat and dry blood and then a roaring voice says:

'That'll be $55.'

And when I open my eyes gasping for air and swallowing gallons of the puddle of beer and everything I see a gold nose ring and red sloppy lips and two gold teeth inside and I recognise the large black cab driver and I sit up slowly holding my head and wait for the singing and swinging to stop and run my fingers over the aching egg on my head and I reach into my bag and dig around while my fumbling fingers pretend to be all thumbs and then I pull out the scrunched-up notes and slowly count out:

Ten twenty thirty forty fifty sixty dollars.

And in a gesture of unprecedented generosity I say:

'You can keep the change,' and hand over the money.

And as I climb out of the cab the driver hands me his card and says:

'Any time you get into trouble you just give me a call OK?' and licks his lips again.

And his gold teeth and big red lips and gold nose ring follow me into the lobby and sit on an occasional table while I buzz Liz's apartment and a voice says:

71

'She's not home.'

Which hits me like the last straw and I start to get a little hysterical and say:

'Listen I've just travelled halfway around the world to see Liz and we have some serious business to discuss and I've got a giant aching egg on my head and concussion and the boss isn't going to be very impressed when he has to collect me from casualty when I collapse and Twentiethcentury Fox's actually an old friend of the family.'

And then the voice says:

'OK you can come up.'

In the lift I'm so uptight and confused and hysterical and nervous that I can't even remember what went through my mind so all of that's edited out and deeply repressed and censored.

And then I'm squeezing into Liz's dark dusty dirty brown apartment and the word—

Flea-bitten—

Flies around inside my head and the gold teeth and the big red lips and the nose ring try to sneak in behind me but I quickly turn around and shoo them away and someone offers me a seat on a creaky slashed badly sprung vinyl sofa-bed and I sort of collapse and my tongue lolls around for a while and then everything seems to melt down and shrivel and become prunish and all the lies I was going to tell Liz evaporate into a dusty powder that makes my nose itch and I sneeze and I notice how airless the air is in Liz's apartment and taste particles of soot on my tongue and the savoury ones remind me how hungry I am and I yawn because I can't seem to get enough air.

And then there's a loud—

Crack—

As my lips split dryly and then that's when the concussion hits me again and bright sparks whiz by and tiny dots dance and dazzle and lurid lights flash on and off and I hear the distant roar as a dozen space shuttles fire up their engines just prior to lift-off and I'm back in a humming place of less than no dreams and God knows what Liz's flatmate is thinking as she watches me disintegrate amidst all the other scavenged surplus living sculptures littered around the room but she must throw a ragged stained dust-saturated blanket over me and forget about me because when I wake up I'm under a blanket all alone in the dusty dark.

And that's when I begin to realise the enormity of my mistake and I sit in the dark stunned and brainless wondering what I'm going to do:

Oh God what am I going to do?

And when Liz's flatmate comes home again I ask her about Twentiethcentury Fox and she just shrugs her shoulders and says something about Liz's sister and I blow my gasket:

Whoosh beeeep whoosh ding.

And then I blow it again:

Whoosh whoosh ding beep.

And storm off to the bathroom and lock the door and almost have a breakdown.

Just as Marilyn's remembrance of things past reaches the bit about the living breathing organisms she hears loud voices in the next room but can't understand what they're saying because they're not speaking English although she's sure she hears one of the voices shout:

'Twentiethcentury Fox THE Twentiethcentury Fox you know?'

Marilyn's Almost Terminal New York Adventure

And then a door slams and everything goes quiet and Marilyn picks herself up from the grimy tiles and splashes her face with cold water and pats it dry with toilet paper and stealthily unlocks the door.

marilyn pauses in the flaking paint doorway and listens to the distant buzzing whirring of an anonymous electrical appliance and even though she wants to stride out boldly and confidently to confront Liz about Twentiethcentury something about the quality of the air holds her back and Marilyn notices that it's stale and tired and over-agitated and thinks:

This air's so dry and stale and tired and there doesn't seem to be any oxygen in it and it seems to be all soot and lead and carbon monoxide and it's like if the air's cold then it gets heated and if it's hot then it gets cooled and all the time it's being churned round and round and why doesn't anyone just leave the air alone for a minute so it can sit quiet and still? I feel like I'm suffocating in this dry airless heat and all the agitation's beginning to get on my nerves.

And her breath comes in fast shallow gasps and as Marilyn tiptoes dizzily through the living room of seemingly secret telephones and hidden light switches past scavenged surplus living sculptures and the creaky slashed badly sprung vinyl sofa-bed she begins to suspect that Liz isn't Twentiethcentury's housekeeper or wife or even ex-wife or ex-girlfriend and even before she sees the icy colony of cockroaches in the freezer she almost makes up her mind once and for all that Liz doesn't know Twentiethcentury Fox because no-one who knows Twentiethcentury Fox could survive

hand-blow-dried

real potato

French fries

in this over-agitated air and this means that International Directory Assistance must have made a mistake when she tried to ring Twentiethcentury from Sydney and as Marilyn takes in the inconsistency of spatial relations the word—

Flea-bitten—

Flies around inside her head and just when she's convinced herself that she is in fact a telecommunications refugee and a victim of International Directory disturbance the anonymous electrical appliance stops whirring and buzzing and Marilyn stands still in a dusty gap between stacks of empty picture frames and her quick shallow breaths fill the room and that's when she decides to try Directory Assistance again because you never know your luck maybe this time she'll get Twentiethcentury's real number so she waits for the anonymous electrical appliance to resume its whirring buzzing and then tiptoes back to the living room her heart in her throat to hunt for seemingly secret telephones and hidden light switches.

Meanwhile Liz wonders about the woman under the ragged stained dust-saturated blanket who keeps moaning:

'Twentiethcentury Fox,' through dry cracked lips and hopes that she isn't one of the shattered wives of one of the businessmen who Liz's sister persists in seducing and that if she is then Liz says a quick quiet prayer that the Twentiethcentury Fox she keeps moaning about isn't THE fabulously wealthy powerful and famous Twentiethcentury Fox everyone else is talking about and imagines the endless law suits and ugly media confrontations and then unflattering front page photos begin to race around in her mind and Liz casts herself centre stage in all the drama as the long-suffering sister left to explain their underprivileged childhood and to tell the moving story of their desperate struggle to make it in the big city and so Liz fusses around in the kitchen with the icy colony of frozen cockroaches and hides in fleeting fancies trying to avoid meeting the strange woman from God knows where for as long as possible.

And after a brief breathless rummage through the living room Marilyn still can't find a telephone or even a light switch so she abandons the dusty dark and strides confidently and boldly through the dusty gaps between stacks of empty picture frames and amplifiers and opens the kitchen door in one smooth easy gesture and that's when Marilyn first sees Liz and when Liz first sees Marilyn without the ragged stained dust-saturated blanket and Marilyn stands still and Liz stands still and their eyes meet and swim across the dusty room and Marilyn's first nervous and cautious impressions of Liz result in speculation rather than conversation and Marilyn thinks—

Wow—

Speculatively and lets her eyes run up and down the short dark woman in the white one-size-fits-all T-shirt and running shoes who's standing in front of an open window where snow and soot blow greasily against the window in the apartment block next door and in one hand the woman is holding a pair of dull stainless steel tongs and the tongs are clamped around a single slice of golden brown recently fried potato and Marilyn thinks:

Wow she actually bothers to make real chips from real potatoes and fries them herself and she's obviously the sort of person who would never use those French fries made from reconstituted potatoes which have been poured into moulds and then frozen and shipped halfway around the world and then defrosted and then deep-fried in second-hand oil and never allowed to dry properly.

And Marilyn nods her head in silent this-is-more-like-it appreciation and lets her eyes wander over to the woman's other hand which is holding a large grimy antiquated hairdryer and then Marilyn looks up into Liz's dark gypsy eyes and smiles a nice-to-meet-you smile and Liz smiles back it's-a-pleasure and switches on the hairdryer and aims it at the golden brown recently fried slice of potato and then puts the fried dried potato chip on a paper towel to drain with all the other hand-blow-dried real potato French fries and then she offers Marilyn the tray and says:

'Would you like some breakfast?'

And Marilyn lets her eyes hover around the small bottle of virgin press olive oil while hours of neglected hunger pains swell inside her and her life-long quest for exotic culinary delights culminates in a feverish burning desire to try some of Liz's hand-blow-dried real potato French fries but she holds herself back and decides she has to know about Liz and Twentiethcentury once and for all so she tears her eyes from the small green bottle and looks Liz boldly in the eyes and says:

'How do you know Twentiethcentury Fox?'

And Liz drops the grimy antiquated hairdryer and grabs a large meat cleaver which she waves about in the dry stale air in front of Marilyn's face and screeches in a high-pitched nasal voice:

'Are you the woman who's been making all the long distance phone calls?'

And for a few minutes they're both frozen like this Liz

waving the large meat cleaver inches from Marilyn's face and brandishing the dull stainless steel cooking tongs in her other hand and Marilyn staring boldly into Liz's eyes trying to stop her eyebrows from flinching having completely lost her desire for exotic culinary delights and then suddenly all the tension and hysteria explodes in unrestrained laughter and it all starts with Marilyn's eyebrows which start trembling and twitching and eventually flinch uncontrollably from all the invisible blows and Liz sees Marilyn's face flinching out of control and starts laughing and then Marilyn gives up on her eyebrows and decides to just let them twitch and starts laughing as well and pretty soon they're both eating hand-blow-dried real potato French fries dipped in Liz's homemade chilli sauce and Liz says chattily:

'You know I've got this big black BMW bike that I can't even afford to drive except to take it out once a week just to recharge the batteries and things have been pretty insecure for me ever since I quit my job as a film publicist and enrolled in a drama school and now I'm waiting for my lucky break in an Off Off Broadway production and in the meantime I'm working the odd day behind a bookstall at Central Park but really one day you have to come out on my bike with me and I'll give you a little tour of the city.'

And Liz pulls out a bottle of tequila from a cupboard buried behind brown paper bags filled with aluminium cans and refundable plastic bottles and then someone starts playing an old salsa record and Liz's flatmates introduce themselves and everyone eats pistachio nuts and chocolate and it's not long before they've eaten everything edible and drunk everything drinkable and that's when they decide to go out dancing to their favourite club and they decide that Marilyn has to stay with them until she finds her two closest long-lost buddies Virginia and Twentiethcentury and Marilyn thinks:

God it's great to make some real friends at last.

Then they all stumble out of the hot dry apartment with its stale tired over-agitated air into the busy chilly sloshy snow street and as they zigzag through the streaming crowds Marilyn mumbles a lot of vague and insignificant tourist observations to herself like:

Wow look at that building that's really postmodern.

And:

I wish we had all these coloured lights on the streets in Sydney.

And almost trips over a pile of black garbage bags which are lying waiting to be collected all over the foot-path as she cranes her neck to see the tippy tops of all the very very tall buildings and at one stage they all stop at the corner of an Avenue and a Street and Marilyn carefully looks in all directions at once trying to work out which direction all the cars are going to come from and while they're all standing waiting to cross the Avenue Marilyn stares up at a building with a pretty decorative orna-mental spire and a young man with glasses and a trench coat says:

'That's the Chrysler Building,' and raises his eye-brows at her before disappearing into the traffic and Marilyn is instantly excruciatingly embarrassed and looks around quickly to make sure Liz and her flat-mates didn't notice and then Marilyn stops looking at the buildings and starts looking at the people and for a moment it seems as if she's nowhere and every-where all at once because the people are all so different and she mumbles something like:

'Who are all these people?'

And Liz and her flatmates gradually leak out the little secrets that add up to years of city life and immeasurable amounts of hard-won bitter and twisted experience and say:

'Puerto Ricans.'

'West Indians.'

'Haitians.'

'Dominicans.'

And Liz laughs and presses Marilyn's arm and says:

'Latinos.'

And then the list goes on:

Afro-Americans.

Koreans.

Chinese.

Thais.

Vietnamese.

Filipinos.

Ecuadorians.

Panamanians.

Senegalese.

Second generation Russians.

Germans.

Poles.

Irish Americans.

Swedes.

And the list goes on and on as they march all over the giant grid until they finally arrive at a dimly lit doorway on a narrow cobblestone street and Liz smiles and talks to the Door and Marilyn looks at the large tarnished knocker and for a while it's as if they'll never get out of the cold cold wind and as the Arctic gale sweeps along the grimy polished cobblestones it collides with a woman huddled inside a giant-sized extra-strength black garbage bag wrapped in layer upon layer of soggy soiled newspapers and urine-and-booze-sodden rags and Marilyn is just about to point out the woman's semi-prostrate form and ask if all of the garbage bags have people living in them when suddenly the door yawns open sucking everybody in and Marilyn is plunged into the hot stale air where they are buffeted by brassy blasts and wildly beating drums and the roof is very low and the bar seems miles away across the crowded room and everyone is wearing black and some people are young but most people are older and everyone is talking fast and laughing and thigh slapping and having a great time even though the band hasn't actually started yet.

And someone nearby yells in Marilyn's ear:

'Can I get you a drink?'

And Marilyn says:

'Sure.'

And then watches as the tall swaying form slowly picks its way through the moving mall of sweaty faces and Liz presses her face close to Marilyn's and yells something about the line-up which involves one very familiar big name and a lot of polysyllabic names which roll off her tongue with great flair and style and Marilyn lets her eyes drift over the sea of moon-faces and one face leads to another and soon she finds herself thinking about the one person whose face she can no longer remember in any detail and hopes against all probability that Twentiethcentury will turn up in this noisy crowded room and then she would rush over with all her lies about a fictitious interview oozing oodles of intensely smiling sensuality and irresistible charm.

'See this?' Liz says out of the blue and Marilyn peers around in the blue but can't really see anything so she shrugs and then Liz grabs her hand and guides it up to the back of her head where her dark woolly hair is clasped in a slippery satin bow and Liz wraps Marilyn's fingers around the dry tightly curled extremity and then starts telling her the history of her hair:

'I first started on my hair when I was still a teenager and I wanted to get it straightened so that I looked just like Cleopatra I mean all I really wanted to do was to make myself look like anyone but my mother you know because I started to think that if I look like my mother in the face then I might grow like her in other ways and I've always wanted to look like my sister Rita who's tall and slim.'

And Marilyn's still looking for Twentiethcentury Fox in the smoky blue light and then Liz starts talking about hair colours and Marilyn imagines her platinum blonde with bright red lips and then platinum blonde with tacky dark roots and agrees that Liz's eyebrows would be too dark and furry so then they'd have to be plucked into high smooth arcs to match the hair and sympathises at the idea of having to dye the roots every second day and knows exactly what Liz means when she says:

'And like every time I looked in a mirror or a shop window I was full of oh-my-God-does-it-really-look-that-bad? insecurities.'

Although she begins to feel a little uneasy when Liz tells her about dyeing her eyebrows and the hair on her forearms and when Liz says:

'Because like all I've ever wanted is to be tall and

blonde and blue-eyed like you and you know you're so
lucky to look like you do and have you ever stopped to
think how lucky and how beautiful you are?' Marilyn
breaks out in a prickly sweat all along her neck and
doesn't know what to say because she always feels very
uncomfortable when anybody says anything really personal about her so she takes a noisy slurp of the icy
tequila cocktail from the tall red-haired stranger who's
standing just behind her and keeps brushing his
forearm against hers and then Liz says:

'Anyway one day my hairdresser says:

'"Listen Liz we have to stop the peroxide or else
your hair's going to fall out."

'And then the next day my hair starts breaking in
half and collects in clumps on my shoulders and on my
pillow so I go to a new hairdresser.'

And Marilyn imagines Liz's hair auburn then
mahogany and then blue-black and isn't surprised
when Liz says:

'And then I finally decided to dye it back to the
colour it is now which is from what I can remember
something like my natural colour although I'm not
really sure and see it's so dry and brittle and all my
ends are split.'

And then the band starts up in earnest and Marilyn
nods for a while at Liz's moving lips and the tall man with
the red hair leans very close and says:

'Do you want to dance?'

But Marilyn feels very shy all of a sudden and
ignores him and stares transfixed at the rows of brass
instruments all held by men in black suits and white
shirts and bow ties and out front there are gongs and all
sorts of drums and xylophones and glockenspiels and a

grand piano on one side and an electric piano on the other and there seem to be so many men up there dancing about all singing the words with or without microphones and there's one guy who's younger than everyone else and he's standing to one side and his suit is baggy and his hair is wild and all he seems to be doing is playing the shakers and mouthing the words and dancing and Marilyn stares at his chiselled face with its full lips and then the tall red-haired man gives her another drink and says:

'Hi I'm Cary.'

And then drags her out onto the sweaty dance floor and she doesn't know what to do and her feet seem slow and heavy and she feels too tall and totally unco-ordinated but Cary shows her a few steps and then she manages to copy one from a silkily clad woman who twists and writhes nearby so she mimics this twisting writhing thing and thinks:

Cuándo cuándo cuándo.

And Cary smiles a lot and the stitch in her left side comes and goes and eventually she stops panting and when she is completely soaked in her own precious bodily fluids the band finally takes a break and Cary buys her another drink and she forgets about everything but the music and dancing and having fun.

And pretty soon it's well into the next morning and the band is packing up and the now shirtless percussionists are surrounded by admiring crowds and Cary introduces her to the Cuban percussionist and the Dominican pianist and the big name who turns out to be Dizzy Gillespie and Marilyn smiles and listens and looks around in the dingy light as faces turn and kiss moons for a moment and a sweet smile spreads across her face and Cary tells her about the band he plays sax in Down South and then Liz says:

'Does anyone feel like breakfast?'

And they all wander out into the icy grey light and carefully step around the woman huddled inside the large black garbage bag who's shivering amidst the soggy soiled newspapers and urine-and-booze-sodden rags and their shoes clatter past on the frozen white cobblestones as they stumble deserted streets to an all-night cafe and somewhere between Marilyn's second and third cup of coffee Liz's sister Rita leans across the table and offers her a job as an illegal alien waitress in the up-market French restaurant Downtown where she works and says to turn up at 4.00 p.m. in a black skirt and a white shirt with a pen and a wine knife and to ask for Zanuck the manager who'll give her a quick rundown and even though the pay's lousy she should make $100 a night in tips and Marilyn nods a quick thank you nod and agrees to be there and privately sighs and feels stupid and looks out the window for Twentiethcentury Fox.

not more than a stone's throw away Twentieth-century S. Fox Jnr sits on the toilet high above the noisy stampeding hordes of Wall Street and contemplates the breakfast menu.

And while Marilyn hovers somewhere between coffee and sleep and delicious delirious daydreams Twentiethcentury umms and ahhs between the wholemeal blueberry waffles with strawberry butter and the fried eggs with hash browns and onion rings and makes yet another fruitless attempt to move his bowels but that's when—

Oh man—

For the third time this week his anus contracts with disgust despair and dismay at the predictable proliferation of all things cooked in salt sugar and fat and the deplorable lack of high-fibre low-calorie items—

Fucken rip off—

Only too painfully aware that things would be different if they'd left the hi-fi bran and soya milk as the special of the week.

And Twentiethcentury grunts and snorts in the agitated air and curses his haemorrhoids and high blood pressure in that no-I-never-did-have-my-adenoids-out-

the predictable
proliferation of
all things cooked
in salt sugar
and fat

so-yes-I-guess-I-do-have-a-sinus-condition accent and then belches softly:

'Excuse me,' and abandons his bowels and break-fast with a grunt and pulls up his boxer shorts with a snort and wanders all swollen and stiff over to his Nautilus machine and starts working on his thighs.

And as he breathes out he says:

'I mean a guy sits on his ass all day doing eight-figure deals with haemorrhoids the size of golf balls.'

And in:

'Hanging out of an asshole the size of a pea.'

And out:

'Not to mention shrivelled balls.'

And in:

'And wonders why his blood pressure.'

And out:

'Tends to get a little out of hand.'

And pausing for a moment all tingling thighs he carefully spreads his plump rump evenly over the sweaty padded leather seat as it dawns on him all sunny and crisp that somehow this is all Garbo's fault because she's never taken the trouble to learn how to cook the sorts of things that keep his juices flowing at a fairly rapid healthy pace producing good-sized keepers at regular intervals and then—

Huh—

Twists his neck to one side and—

Crack—

Cracks his neck thoughtfully.

Maybe Garbo is just being stubborn because he'd asked her for a list of names and places and dates of all the people she's ever slept with because ever since then he's noticed that she's been acting a little strange:

I mean like take last night for instance.

And so Twentiethcentury indulges in a little remembrance of things past and begins the inevitable descent into the deep nebulous caverns of sensation where memory flickers and drips in damp limestone caves of recollection.

Wishing a Lot of Why-Me? October-the-Thirteenth Thoughts all Wistful and Cold and Lonely

And Garbo and Charlie and I are all sitting at the bar after work sipping on our margaritas and eating corn chips dipped in hot chilli sauce and like winding down and relaxing and anyway Garbo says to Charlie:

'There's one thing Charlie I've never been able to understand and that is: how do the abstractions of economics relate to something like equities you know?'

And Charlie says:

'Well you see Garbo the abstractions of economics have nothing to do with the stock market.'

And I say:

'Your average broker only understands that whatever goes up must come down and whatever goes down might come up.'

And Garbo just ignores me and smiles at Charlie that smile that always makes me want to bury my face in her dark rich curly hair and I'm kind of pissed at her because of all the crap she's been dragging me through lately like all the jokes about my haemorrhoids and poetry and Charlie's my best friend so I say:

'Anyway Charlie I want to buy a seat you know get a few of us together you me and my brother Warner.'

'You mean Warner the actor?'

'Yeah Warner.'

'Who does what's it called? That Russian acting?'

'Strasberg.'

'Yeah the Strasberg guy Warner huh Warner you think he'd be?'

'Yeah he'd be in on it.'

'I don't know Twentiethcentury a seat with you me and Warner.'

And Garbo must be getting pissed at me now because I'm like monopolising Charlie so she says:

'That's what I mean Charlie like what's a seat?'

And then I say real calm:

'A seat to trade.'

And Charlie's still not sure what's going on not being as familiar with her antics as I am and he says:

'You buy a seat it's not an actual seat but it enables you to trade you know?'

And Garbo says with her cleavage:

'To trade equities?'

And Charlie looks over at me and says:

'Yeah.'

Slowly I then say:

'Anyway Charlie I had a look into equities the other day and I kind of miss it you know?'

'I thought you were glad to get out of equities?'

'You can be glad but still miss things about it.'

But Garbo won't give up and says:

'But what exactly are equities? You know in concrete terms?'

And she says this with that smile again at Charlie and heaves her cleavage and God knows what Charlie's thinking and I'm just thinking:

Huh bummer of the week: there goes another relationship.

But somehow I deal with it and just sit back and wait for Charlie to leave so we can talk and get things off our chests and Charlie keeps looking at me still not sure what's going on and then he says:

'Alfred's really getting interested in the market he's aah taken a job at MGM.'

'We kept all the brokers at MGM when we took them over.'

'Yeah MGM are the best-trained brokers in the business.'

'Huh there's gotta be a lot of people on the street now though.'

'Yeah huh five thousand.'

'Is Alfred really at MGM?'

'Alfred knows nothing about the stock market.'

'I'm getting more interested in it.'

And all the time I'm just watching her and feeling sorry for myself even though I should be feeling good after making big $$$ at work but then I guess when a relationship goes down the tube you can expect to feel a little pissed and it's kind of like an important client's left a bombshell on the computer by signing up with the competition leaving you looking like just another one-time Wall Street powerhouse you know what I mean? And like with my history of broken hearts the sharks of Wall Street never looked so tame.

And then Charlie leans over and says in his best Saratoga Racetrack sleaze:

'My boss is the next guy to go down for insider trading.'

And all I can say is:

'Oh yeah? huh,' not really interested and hoping Charlie notices I'm not but meanwhile he goes on

talking unable to stop:

'Yeah I mean I shouldn't be telling you this because I shouldn't even know but—'

And all I can think about is Garbo and how she's just the latest casualty in a long history of broken hearts and then you know there was the time like when I asked her for a list of names and places and dates of all the people she'd ever slept with on the advice of my attorney because you know you just can't be too careful these days and Garbo just stands up and storms out leaving me feeling pretty inadequate and anyway Charlie finally picks up the vibes and leaves and then Garbo leans over across the table forcing me to notice how many buttons she's undone and smiles that smile that makes me want to bury my face in her dark rich curly hair and says:

'I'm sorry honey I can't make it for dinner tonight so why don't we take a raincheck till tomorrow and meet at that little up-market French restaurant Downtown for a late-night snack OK?'

And then she stands up on my reluctant sigh and brushes her lips lightly across my seven o'clock shadow and I just stare as she leaves and everyone else sort of watches too and I feel really stupid at the bar all alone so I leave and go home thinking a lot of poetic thoughts and singing a bit of Bob Dylan to myself and wishing a lot of why-me? October-the-thirteenth thoughts all wistful and cold and lonely.

And at this point in Twentiethcentury's remembrance of things past he sighs a deep snotty time-to-cut-my-losses sigh and slides off his Nautilus and pads back through luscious pile to his private can where he drops his boxer shorts again and begins to make weary calculations of:

    information flows
    internal audits
    real values
    assets and liabilities
    limited partnerships
    tax benefits
    employee benefits
    high water marks
    team strategies
    COMEX interests
    insurance deposit conversions
    and:
    weakened loan demands.

And idly wonders if he'll ever see the reckless sum he sunk in herbal vinegar again this side of the financial year.

But somehow Twentiethcentury's financial speculations always seem to lead to biological obsessions like today's question of the shit that never was and then words slide out and settle on the carpeted floor resplendent in their no-I-never-did-have-my-adenoids-out-so-yes-I-do-have-a-sinus-condition accent:

'I mean we're in the middle of a pretty dicey deal here and all I can think about is whether or not I remembered to insert my fucken suppository this morning?

'I mean a guy shoves all that fatty shit in one end and then shoves drugs in the other end and wonders why things fuck up occasionally.

'I mean like if you don't eat you don't shit you know? And if you don't shit you die I mean really it's that simple.

'Crap is good you know it's necessary like it's probably the most underrated activity known to modern man.'

While Twentiethcentury massages his stomach and cracks his neck Garbo sits staring at her screen in her noisy Madison Avenue office while his gruffly grunted words play over and over in her mind:

You know I'd really appreciate it if you'd make a list of names and places and dates of all the people you've ever slept with including surnames because you know like you just can't be too careful these days.

And Garbo wonders not for the first time through smeary mascara'd lashes how this shrewd cold fish Wall Street type can also write such moving and raging bull sensitive poetry and thinking about poetry she pulls out a worn and wrinkled sheet of baby-blue personally monogrammed paper that she always keeps in the inside pocket of her 14-carat-and-crocodile-skin purse and reads from the childish script she knows by heart:

> *Darling Garbo,*
>
> *You didn't need to spell it out*
> *I knew what was occurring*
> *I ask myself: who is in charge?*
> *Your Goethe—my Goering?*
>
> *Moments connect, time slows and stops*
> *I hope there is no victor:*
> *Oh black hole open up: abyss!*
> *(There is no scale Herr Richter.)*
>
> *Your gentle touch: my hair's a mess*
> *Oh no! Not this again!*
> *And wait the day immortal words:*
> *Please can't we still be friends?*

Flee daunting thought not to return
I say: there'll be no battle,
To have the spoils and miss the rest
That would not test our mettle.

These kisses last and linger on
As searching eyes all gleam and shine,
In love-stuck gaze all chat and talk
Yet, silence best we do divine.

When meaning comes and leaves all time
Each pindrop gaze it seems anew
Less strangers now—and less is more
And more, like me and you.

Twentiethcentury S. Fox Jnr

And Garbo sits very quietly and sniffles and wishes she'd been able to find the path beyond Twentieth-century's gruff and grunting exterior to touch his raging bull sensitive poet's heart but somehow everything she says comes out wrong —

Sniff sniff—

Because whenever she's tried she's always sounded abrupt and aggressively independent or nosy and vindictive and she's sick of dragging herself over hot coals about her inability to open up and open him up and free their relationship from its stagnant repressive insecurity so she straightens her shoulder pads and sweeps her stray rich dark curls from her moist and gluggy lashes and then carefully and decisively folds the baby-blue personally monogrammed paper and places it back into the inside pocket of her 14-carat-and-crocodile-skin purse and summons all her angry resolve to think determined thoughts like:

Names and places and dates for Christsakes of all the people I've ever slept with?

And:

I mean is he talking about one-night stands like Mailer or Arthur or does he draw the line at one week or does he only want LTRs?

And she scratches a rough patch on her heavily pancaked cheek and thinks:

Because I can count my Long Term Relationships on one hand like there's:

The Beatles

Grant

Hitchcock and

Jack.

And Elvis I guess although Elvis's a bit more of a borderline case I mean something that's so up and down and off and on can't really be an LTR especially seeing we never even went to bed I mean technically to bed you know?

Scratch scratch.

Why do I find myself craving hot pastrami on rye? Was that Hitchcock's idea of breakfast or The Beatles' idea of a midnight snack?

And while she tries to concentrate on tomorrow morning's deadline for her 'I Was Wrong About Penis Envy: Extracts From Freud's Secret Diary' article she's really thinking:

As if I could ever marry anyone with an anal fixation and haemorrhoids the size of golf balls even if he is a sensitive unpublished poet? I mean how could I even subliminally think of marriage at this point in my career? Especially like to someone whose idea of a romantic morning is a session on the can that produces the ultimate shit and then gives ultimatums on the basis of legal advice about sexually transmitted diseases?

Holy shit!

But then I guess he has a point because someone like Jack is definitely in the high-risk category especially after his addiction and everything even though he swears he never used a needle I guess there's always the possibility that he's lying I mean you know what they say about addictive personalities and manipulation and deception you know? like addicts even lie to themselves: but then I still think it's none of his goddamn business and I don't want any lawyers or private detectives knowing my personal history and if Twentiethcentury really wants to find out he's just going to have to go and get tested himself because if he wants to use all this as an excuse to ruin a perfectly good relationship well I'm certainly not going to stop him.

And then Garbo twirls one of her dark rich curls around a delicate pearl pink fingertip:

I mean if you don't eat you don't shit you know? and if you don't shit you die.

All haunted and sniffling and determined to be alone.

after the fourth cup of coffee Marilyn and Liz and her flatmates stumble home in the white snowy cold and Marilyn kisses Cary goodbye and takes his personally monogrammed card and yes she'll call him some time and she almost enjoys her first gasp of the dry stale tired over-agitated air back in Liz's apartment after all the icy watery-eyed feet-freezing cold and col-lapses—

Aah—

On the creaky slashed badly sprung vinyl sofa-bed and snuggles—

Mmm—

Under the dirty stained dust-saturated blanket and falls asleep as soon as her head hits the pillow and has dreams about Virginia and mummies' curses and being trapped inside tombs full of biting mosquitoes and that's why Marilyn wakes up the next day and wonders:

What on earth's happened to Virginia?

And immediately imagines the worst:

Oh no.

Because Marilyn doesn't know that when Virginia fails to appear at the airport at the last minute it's not because she elopes with someone with cellulite high blood pressure and asthma who's

one of those
once-in-a-lifetime
employment
opportunities

middle aged and rich and whose artistic pretensions
conceal humble origins or because she surrenders to
alcoholic fixations and phantasmagorical hallucinations and
kills herself with a standing knife or because she falls
madly in love with Lawrence and is celebrating with a
bottle of French champagne now that Marilyn's left the
country or because she receives secret information about a
hijacking or a bomb implantation or a faulty seal in an
emergency exit door.

Marilyn doesn't know that Virginia fails to appear at
the airport at the last minute because a certain Mr
Grove Weidenfeld sends her an unbidden summons for
one of those once-in-a-lifetime employment opportunities
just hours before their planned departure to New
York.

It all starts when Virginia arrives home after spending
hours waiting in Casualty to have her wrists bandaged
and she finds a hand-delivered letter slipped under the
door and calls out:

'Hi Marilyn.'

But there's no answer because Marilyn's gone home
and is lying on her bed dreaming about being mugged by
an elephant in Central Park so Virginia sits down to
read the letter which says:

> *Dear Virginia,*
>
> *I have been studying your work for
> some time and I believe you possess the
> necessary qualifications to fulfil a vacant
> position in my unique organisation. You
> will be assigned an endless variety of
> seemingly random tasks. Understanding
> your love of all things mysterious bizarre*

and enigmatic I will say no more.
I look forward to meeting you later
this afternoon.
Yours sincerely,
Mr Grove Weidenfeld.

And Grove's letter speaks to Virginia like the voice of God because every word seems brighter and more brilliant and more colourful and more defined than any of the words she's seen before indeed the words comprising Grove's letter are so crystal clear they could almost be the words of an American and while anybody else would probably be suspicious about this unsolicited interview Virginia welcomes the mysterious bizarre enigmatic missive with open I've-spent-my-whole-life-waiting-for-something-like-this-to-happen arms and she nods in this-is-more-like-it appreciation and looks up in wonder and thanks for this deliverance out of the blue and Virginia goes into an absorbing introspective trance that is several extremely satisfying hours long where she speculates whether her new job will have anything to do with strange urban myths or gossip columns or any of the good things in life but then—

Oh oh—

And that's when Virginia realises that she's left Marilyn standing lost alone and confused in the departure lounge wondering and waiting and so Virginia clamps her eyes tightly shut and shouts telepathically:

Just board the flight without me.

And photo-kinetically propels Marilyn through the airport gate and onto the plane.

Meanwhile Grove Weidenfeld sits at the kitchen table surrounded by a familiar unmistakable hyper-real glow and finishes his second packet of unfiltered Camels for the day between puffs of his ventilator spray and draws up an outline for Virginia's big assignment waiting impatiently for her to knock at his door so he can find out whether he's done it again and hit the jackpot or whether he's done it again and it's back to the drawing board.

And while it's blatantly obvious from Grove's physical presence that he has cellulite high blood pressure and asthma and is middle aged and out of condition that is also all most people know about him because Grove's the sort of person who believes a past is worth guarding well into the future and so has to be taken at face value when he says:

'Like I'm really into anthropological research and I mean like the human condition you know like TV and architecture and supermarkets and satellites and pop music and homemade videos and vegetarian food.'

And when Virginia finally twirls into Grove's lounge room he almost falls head over heels backwards in holy-shit-I've-done-it-again shock because he realises quick as a flash that she's perfect for the job and as tears of joy begin to prickle the corners of his eyes in an almost American kind of way he attempts to keep calm and rearranges his chins and makes subtle adjustments to his posture but that's when he starts to hear the happy tinkle of coins tumbling out of a slot machine in a noisy I've-just-hit-the-jackpot rush and suddenly his chest tightens and he begins to wheeze and Virginia stands there her hand outstretched and her beady-eyed smile all frozen and frosty while Grove plunges his fumbling fingers through coat pockets and desk drawers and through trousers and shirts until he

102

remembers in a neon flash of colossal magnitude that his spray is still where he left it this morning after breakfast between his first packet of Camels for the day and an empty box of Coco Pops and he rushes out of the room wheezing and gasping almost doubled over in pain and panic and Virginia thinks—

Wow—

And rolls her eyes and follows him lamely to the kitchen where Grove stands pounding his chest holding his breath between gasps from his ventilator spray and whispers:

'Excuse me,' hoarsely and offers Virginia his hand blushing pinkly at his unfortunate social misdemeanour and Virginia smiles and says:

'Hi,' and shakes his soft pudgy hand thinking Grove Weidenfeld is almost like an American soap opera star but not quite.

Minutes later Grove gloats from the other side of the coffee table and says:

'I mean like if there's one thing Virginia I know a lot about that's people and if I'm as right about you as I think I am then—'

And on and on and so on and Virginia thinks:

How corny.

And begins to wish she'd gone to New York with Marilyn.

But then when Grove says:

'I know you're probably beginning to wish you'd gone to New York with Marilyn but I happen to know you're going to love working with me so if you'll just bear with me here maybe I can change your mind OK?'

And smiles across the coffee table Virginia smiles back and nods touché and wonders about this

Australian businessman in his badly cut brown suit and his mauve and brown striped tie and his beige shirt and vinyl belt with a tarnished gold buckle and coffee brown socks and rust brown shoes and his $25 Swatch watch and ponytail disguised as a smooth talking almost American and Virginia becomes so introspectively absorbed she's only half listening as Grove rambles on about calluses:

'And like after hours and hours at this microfiche you know flipping through files and looking up references I notice like my hands are covered in these fucken lumps these calluses and I'm thinking like—'

But Virgina's ears do prick up and her attention does zero in and her thoughts finally do come into focus as soon as Grove starts to talk about research and so Virginia listens very closely while Grove explains that research is always a bit of a gamble in that you try and try and nothing happens and there's no pay-out and then all of a sudden:

'Bingo you know?'

And Virginia looks back at Grove and lets her beady eyes sparkle wide open oyster-eyed surprise under a single raised eyebrow and that's when Grove fixes her with one of his dark brooding stares of understanding and gets to the point:

'Yeah like I take photos and I'm also an art dealer and I manage a couple of rock bands and I like to think of myself as a man with his fingers in many pies but this new line of research I'm planning is something different altogether and I mean like I think at this stage we should discuss and see if we agree on several delicate ethical matters.'

So Virginia nods and narrows her eyes beadily as

Grove goes on to suggest in meandering words and hints and grunts that she'll be expected to:

kind of crash people's conversations,

and:

invade their privacy,

and:

like undertake slightly unethical methods of research.

And Virginia wonders:

Is he psycho perverted crazy or CIA?

And meanwhile Grove's explaining her first assignment:

'So you'll have to carry this small but like hi-fidelity reel to reel in some kind of leather bag and you turn up at the specified place at the specified time and like you're going to love this part then you attempt to record I mean to capture all the like all the significant environmental sounds as well as making some kind of comprehensive sampling of as many different conversations as possible.'

And during Grove's recital he doesn't stay still and in between instructions and explanations he stands up and sits down and stands ups again and sits down again and Virginia can't help noticing that the jacket of the brown Australian businessman's suit is cut just a little too small around the chest and the pants are too long and sag at the waist and she's finally just about to confront him about who he really works for when Grove says:

'Look I know you're wondering who I really am and who I work for and all I can say is that like I'm not who I appear to be at all and so you're right there and I mean I work for myself and I might be just a little crazy and perverse and yeah what you'll be doing will be a little bit like spying.'

And Grove shrugs:

'So.'

And leaves saying:

'Excuse me I'll be right back,' over his shoulder.

Virginia sighs a mystified what-have-I-got-to-lose sigh and peers under the bandages on her wrists and suspects that Grove knows all about her hours in Casualty and probably knows all about Marilyn as well and probably knows about what happened with her mother and everything and wonders why she doesn't feel outraged at the thought of being spied on and probably bugged and followed and can't help feeling vaguely flattered by the idea and she smiles to herself and that's when—

Oh my God—

Grove comes back wearing a pair of Dr Marten's boots and gold and black bicycle shorts and a big baggy black T-shirt and his hair's loose and greasy and Virginia notices the way this changes the shape of his face and everything seems rounder and there's something very strange about the bulging cellulite and flabby muscle but Virginia's not quite sure what and meanwhile Grove is smoking an unfiltered Camel wheezing audibly and says:

'There's just one more thing that I have to make absolutely clear to you Virginia and like that is that you may have to risk losing everything on this assignment I mean like friends family you name it because I mean you may have to almost disappear completely if you know what I mean I mean really totally disappear for good like there's no coming back like that's it like dead like disappear in a really ultimate and final way get it?'

And Grove broods over her bandaged wrists and then slowly drags his eyes up to her face and Virginia concentrates on his pockmarked chin and the blackheads on his nose and the tiny burst blood vessels around his eyes before she lets him fix her with another one of his dark brooding stares of understanding and Grove begins to break out in holy-shit-I've-done-it-again goose bumps and his breath begins to come in gasps as his chest tightens and just before he starts to hear the happy tinkle of coins tumbling out of a slot machine he stands up suddenly and Virginia stands up and they shake hands awkwardly and Virginia feels she should say something like:

'Thanks,' but can't take her eyes off the cellulite and flab and Grove puts his arm around her shoulder in a friendly farewell embrace but almost burns her with his cigarette and they both laugh nervously and just before he ushers her through the door he fixes her with another dark brooding stare of understanding and says:

'Don't envy balls Virginia break them.'

And suddenly she's out in the dazzling afternoon sun with the howling cicadas and a leather shoulder bag and a tiny hi-fidelity reel to reel as the door closes quietly behind her.

And this is how in just 17 minutes Virginia's long and short term plans are irrevocably altered and as she makes her way home to prepare herself for her first conversation-crashing assignment she feels that a new world is opening up before her and that things are suddenly infinitely more interesting and exciting than ever before and that things are everything that TV should be and that Grove or whoever he really is is the most fascinating person she's ever met and little thrills of excitement trill inside her at the idea of the fee which she's sure lies somewhere near the beating heart of the matter and she's only too peachy keen to find out exactly how financially viable her unethical conversation crashing will be.

But what exactly does he mean by:

Almost disappear completely?

Virginia thinks she understands what he means but then she also hopes he doesn't mean what she understands him to mean because if she's understood what she understands him to mean correctly then as far as she can understand they share a pretty bleak understanding of the future which amounts to a mutual understanding between them that she mightn't have one.

And she's still wondering about what she understands and what she doesn't understand when she arrives at her first conversation-crashing assignment and her beady eyes harden with purpose and her palms itch sweatily amongst her restless fingers and her mouth is firmly set beneath her beaky nose in her long lined face and she's suddenly inside a small white private art gallery where the cheap nasty champagne has been lined up in neat rows along a white clothed trestle table and the black diamanté-studded strutting forms provide a dramatic visual backdrop for the bright witty conversation and Virginia consults Grove's precise instructions and stealthily switches the concealed recording device on and off and shuffles around the room in a large figure eight just like Grove suggests and when she gets back to the beginning she switches the device off and she's just about to leave when she notices the arresting oh-no-it's-not-another-Tutankhamenexhibition standing lamp with its gold and lapis lazuli studded pharaoh's coffin complete with mosaics and hieroglyphics and as Virginia stares into the flashing narrow eyes she feels a cold ominous chill of death pass right through her as the words —

Almost disappear completely —

Tape loop in her mind and without looking around she steps sideways and backwards to the door and Virginia doesn't stop running till she arrives home panting and lambent.

And she reads the next set of instructions from Grove all trembling fingers and gulping scotch:

> *Dear Virginia,*
>   *Congratulations and guess what? I'm sending you to LA oh and could you please send me the first tape before you leave?*
>   *Grove.*

And slaps the glass down:

Aah.

The flight leaves in a matter of minutes and she's just about to seal the tape in the postpack when she's overcome by callused-researcher curiosity and guiltily plays the tape first and this is what she hears:

'. . . very fetishistic . . .'

'. . . and Chaplin said don't . . .'

'. . . they're very fleshy lips don't you think?'

'. . . must be priceless . . .'

'. . . elegant calm yet breathing with life . . .'

'. . . I just don't understand what . . .'

'. . . how's your flat going?'

109

'. . . photographer from *Vogue* magazine can I take your . . .'

'. . . at the Royal Necropolis . . .'

'. . . like unguents and precious oils . . .'

But the disembodied floating phrases only send more cold chills down her spine so she switches off the tape and throws a few things in a bag and rushes out into the warm summer night.

As soon as Virginia slumps down into her roomy first-class seat she slips soporific into a deep dreamless sleep and when she wakes up hours later the plane is circling LA airport restless and predatory and Virginia mumbles:

'Wow,' into the made-for-Hollywood sunset as the plane plunges down into the orange haze of the dust bowl and her lungs involuntarily contract and suddenly she can't seem to get enough air and the space-age highways and tall ghostly buildings loom close and Virginia thinks:

What would happen if we landed on the wrong runway? Is this what he means by almost disappear completely?

And breaks out in a cold sweat and gasps and grasps the sides of her seat and closes her eyes and it's only once the plane is finally taxiing across the tarmac that she opens her eyes and says:

'I wish I was flying Qantas.'

Grove's next flawless instructions lead her to a blue plastic seat near a souvenir shop somewhere in the labyrinth of LA international airport and as Virginia sits and switches she's gradually lulled into a false sense of security by the soothing flow of people and she begins to suspect that her research will inevitably lead her to Marilyn and that city that out-cities all other cities and Virginia is only vaguely surprised when Grove directs her to a cubicle in the women's toilets and while she sits and switches she assumes that her recordings must be picking up some more elusive sound than the conversation of the two women at the mirror and Virginia imagines that this elusive sound is probably something like a distant phone call or the flight arrangements of another passenger or maybe even the sound of approaching footsteps or a whispered exchange and she's just beginning to think of herself as a spy when the PA belches her name into the white-tiled space and she almost jumps guiltily out of her skin as she makes her way through waves of nail-biting anxiety to the Casablanca Restaurant on the mezzanine level.

And she's not even slightly surprised when she sees another postage prepaid package sitting on one of the tinted glass window tables and as she reads through Grove's next meticulous instructions she's reassured by the hefty wad of US currency and the two airline tickets only seem to confirm her suspicions that she's on her way to Marilyn and that city of cities and then she reads Grove's next note:

> Dear Virginia,
>   The first tape is excellent although I would appreciate it if you made your movements more fluid in future as the sound quality will improve a little oh and good luck for Washington and by the time you reach New York I think you'll be

> *ready for your first big assignment—*
> *Twentiethcentury S. Fox Jnr. But more*
> *about that later.*
>   *Grove.*

And Virginia is not at all convinced that it's possible to make her movements any more fluid having always been fairly uncoordinated and terrible at things like surfing and sailing and jazz ballet and karate and especially abominable at tai chi and then thinks—

Oh—

Because this means all her assignments so far have been practice runs and she becomes increasingly mystified about what Grove means by a big assignment and wonders if the Twentiethcentury S. Fox Jnr he was talking about in his letter is THE Twentiethcentury Fox of TV fame and can't help wondering a little nail-bitingly when she'll have to almost disappear completely.

And as soon as she makes herself comfortable in yet another roomy first-class seat a lousy hack air hostess noisily slaps down a bottle of chilled dry white wine with a clear plastic cup on a doily'd dish smiling vaguely and Virginia smiles hi and helps herself to the bottle and flicks through newspapers and magazines and lets the hours blur on and the bottle empties and just as she's about to doze off into la la land someone sits down—

Humph—

In the seat next to her and Virginia sees it's the noisy air hostess and smiles in a friendly oh-God-you-must-hate-doing-this way and offers her the last of the wine but the air hostess just shakes her head and starts talking in a dry husky voice at a brisk seemingly artificially stimulated pace and she tells Virginia all about how much she hates being an air hostess and how all she really wants to be is an actress and:

'You know for me it's not so much a case of how much I hate my job so much as how much I hate my JOBS because like my jobs are so casual and I have so many of them that I always end up losing track of who I am and what I do you know and the worst thing about the work I do is that I don't get to see my friends or I wouldn't get to see them if I had any you see I don't have any friends actually I don't have a life outside of these goddamn awful fucking jobs that I hate doing and now the situation has gone from bad to worse because I'm madly in love with this Ostralian guy who's like a bit of a hairy snail and has eyes like a possum and I'm actually thinking about quitting work altogether so that I can have a relationship because if I don't stop all this flying around for all these stupid rip-off airlines I'll never have a relationship at all and isn't that a lousy deal having to choose between life and work but that's the way it seems to me and doesn't life suck?'

And the voice drones on and on but Virginia doesn't notice because she's dozed off into la la land and the next thing Virginia does notice has nothing to do with the air hostess who's given up on Virginia and already moved on in search of her next victim.

In other words the first thing Virginia notices upon awakening are Grove's puzzling parting words which are flying around and around in sickening seesaw circles inside her head.

What on earth did he mean by:

Don't envy balls Virginia break them?

113

marilyn snuggles under the dirty stained dust-saturated blanket on the creaky slashed badly sprung vinyl sofa-bed and wonders:

Where am I?

And coughs all scratchy throat and itchy nose in the dry tired over-agitated air.

And as she sits up slowly one eye cracks grimily open and then the other eye opens dry and puffy and the scavenged surplus living sculptures take their shadowy shapes in the lounge room of seemingly secret telephones and hidden light switches and she's not really sure where she's going as she staggers to the bathroom with the no-longer-phenomenal sink with no plug thinking lots of we're-all-slowly-suffocating-to-death thoughts.

And Marilyn locks the door carefully and leans over the sink and splashes and foams when suddenly she hears a high rasping voice and Marilyn instantly aborts her ablutions and clings to the sink in I-don't-know-how-much-more-of-this-I-can-take white-knuckled desperation while everything begins to pulsate and swim in a psychedelic swirl of loud and leering colours and her head spins and

a very nice

slightly-bucked-

teeth-with-

calcium-spots

smile

wobbles woozy and out of control.

So Marilyn settles on her safe settled-beneath-the-cistern seat and leans back and lets her eyes stick to the dust on the light fittings and murmurs:

'Twentiethcentury,' all weary and whimsical and she can't remember his beneath-the-appearance self or the jaded world-weary look about his face and even though Twentiethcentury seems lost in layers of smoggy snow and sloshy tequila cocktails she knows she's going to meet him somehow anyway and she's just about to try Directory Assistance again when the high rasping voice says:

'Marilyn before you go his phone number starts with 935 and the other digits are yours for a small fee.'

And Marilyn freezes and there's a loud—

Thud—

As her heart skips a beat and even though she's still trying to ignore Little Johnny Wayne she can't help stopping dead in her tracks and saying:

'What was that Little Johnny?'

But Little Johnny Wayne's probably sulking in a pipe somewhere and doesn't answer and Marilyn starts rummaging around in the bathroom cupboard and finds an eyeliner pencil and rips off a piece of generic non-brand toilet paper and says sweetly:

'Little Johnny oh Little Johnny would you mind repeating that number?'

When suddenly there's a loud knock on the door and Marilyn whispers:

'Come on Jack what's the fucken number please?'

But Little Johnny keeps very quiet and still and the knocking gets louder and fiercer and when Marilyn opens the door she thinks—

Oh oh —

Because Liz's flatmate is standing there with a wine knife and Liz calls out:

'Breakfast's ready,' from the other room and that's when Marilyn remembers about working in the up-market French restaurant Downtown so she follows Liz's flatmate out into the lounge room of seemingly secret telephones and hidden light switches which is full of people with black skirts and white shirts and Liz walks around with a tray of hand-blow-dried real potato French fries and frosty foaming cups of egg nog and everything becomes blurred by this creamy brandy breakfast and some time later Marilyn finds herself stumbling along in the sunny snowy paradise of a quiet Downtown street struggling with the nagging persistent voice that keeps saying:

Who are you trying to kid you're not a waitress God you'd be no better than a lousy hack pretending to be a waitress.

But before she can answer back she's already inside the up-market French restaurant Downtown and her shoes squelch mushily as she twirls and whirls across the black and white tiles to the distant expanse of the pinky-grey bar but she never reaches the bar because when she's only halfway there she suddenly feels alone and naked amongst all the black and white crisscrossing strangers and the persistent nagging voice won't leave her alone so she turns on her soggy heel and flees to the friendly snowy paradise of the wintry street as the word:

'Chicken,' slips unbidden from a corner of her lippy mouth.

Seconds later Marilyn stands panting on the corner of

Duane and Reade and just in case anyone's following her she hurries back to the soothing sordid safety of the subway and oblivious to details like Uptown or Downtown she hastily hurdles the turnstile and worms her way into the subway's seething stinky depths.

Even when she's securely stationed and anchored to a slimy silvery pole she still feels woozy and wobbly and looks over her shoulder just in case while guilty thoughts pluck the harpstrings of her heart and a heated debate starts up inside her where all her guilty feelings about Liz and her flatmates do battle with her innermost sense of insecurity and anxiety and thoughts like:

I'll make a terrible waitress I'll just be hopeless and I'll drop things—

Zing and ding with:

But what am I going to say to Liz and her flatmates?

And everything's flying around and making a lot of clanging and banging noise when a derro walks through the car with a smashed-up saxophone and delivers a poetry performance subway style:

> *I'm a musician.*
> *Can't play.*
> *Saxophone is broken.*
> *Got to fix my saxophone.*
> *Jobless is homeless.*
> *But I'm gonna play for you.*
> *But can't play.*
> *Saxophone is broken.*

And then he plays a high-pitched squealing squeak behind his purple glitter glasses and everyone laughs and giggles and then he seems to fix Marilyn with one of his crazy homeless-musician's eyes and starts inching towards her thrusting his cup in her face and Marilyn hears something go—

Snap—

Inside her as she stares at her own terror-struck eyes which are reflected in his purple glasses and she wonders whether he has a knife or a gun or whether he'll just hit her over the head with his sax and just when her eyebrows start flinching out of control from all the imaginary blows the car stops with a jolt at a station and the derro is washed away in a sweeping tide of trench coats hiking boots and glasses and Marilyn slides into a vacant seat and gropes around in her bag for some kind of defence and her fingers seize hold of her spiral notebook and the airline-logoed biro so she opens up to a fresh page and writes:

> *Very cold not sure how cold but warm on crowded subway.*
> *Snow flurries.*
> *Everyone wears trench coats glasses and hiking boots.*

And:

> *Fending off advances from crazy begging derros on subways and now there's a guy in the carriage who keeps staring at me and should I give him a filthy look or start whistling loudly or change carriages?*

And just then a man wearing a trench coat glasses and

119

hiking boots leans over and says:

'Scarves,' and Marilyn stares back at the glasses and raises her eyebrows not sure whether to look interested or hostile and the man just smiles and asks:

'Are you Ostralian?'

Before she can answer he goes on to tell her all about how everyone at work's fighting over who's going to cover the story about the recent Ostralian crocodile plague and that he'd recognise the Ossie accent anywhere and then Marilyn's about to protest that she hasn't said anything yet and gets as far as:

'But I—' when the man goes on to tell her that everyone wears trench coats glasses hiking boots and scarves and that scarves are a very important item and that she should look very closely into scarves and start wearing one herself especially once it really starts snowing and gets really cold and that there's just one other item she has to pay attention to and Marilyn says:

'What's that?'

And he says:

'Detail.'

And then he goes on to tell her that a writer must always pay a lot of careful attention to detail and that she's made a bit of a mistake in singling out trench coats because if she looks around with a writerly eye for detail she'll see that there are as many people wearing trench coats as there are wearing overcoats and Marilyn nods in agreement and stares at his crooked teeth as he raves for a few minutes about gloves and mittens and muffs and when he's finished she says:

'Teeth.'

And he says:

'53rd and Fifth have you seen the Jackie Gleeson retrospective yet?'

As they worm and wriggle from car to station to steps to street he opens her eyes to detail with a fairly incessant stream of observations about shoes scarves gloves glasses and coats and explains with an air of practised defiance and seemingly self-mocking pomposity that he never wears hiking boots no matter how cold it gets and he never wears jeans and just about always wears a tie and then he gets to his teeth and blames his years spent in English boarding schools for his crooked teeth and then Marilyn says:

'I've always really loved odd teeth.'

And suddenly they're in the lobby of a large imposing museum where he says looking over his shoulder:

'I'm really sorry I've got to go I've got a deadline you know?'

And then he shakes her hand and suggests they meet for lunch some time and she nods and then he hands her a card which reads:

R. HUDSON
749-2404

And loosening his scarf R. what-the-fuck-does-the-R.-stand-for? Hudson disappears into the mass of heavily overcoated well-heeled patrons and Marilyn notices that she should have been at work ten minutes ago and in an attempt to counteract the rising wave of anxiety beginning in her icy frozen toes she plunges into the muted throng and dissolves into multiplicity and is carried along to the collection of dinosaur art.

And while she stands transfixed before a pictorial representation of macabre and excessive violence a tall

121

thin man wearing a bright red scarf and a navy cashmere overcoat and black Italian slip-ons and tortoiseshell glasses sidles up to her and asks:

'Do you think it's a painting or a poster?'

And Marilyn turns towards the red scarf and the rosy cheeks of a pale complexion where vibrant blue eyes glitter behind their speckly brown rims and then she peers very closely and sincerely at the pictorial representation of macabre and excessive violence until she detects the brush strokes and then she says:

'I think it's a painting.'

Followed by:

'See the brush strokes?'

And pointing:

'There.'

And he nods his head from the upper reaches of his tall spindly sapling height and asks:

'Are you from Ostralia?'

And then he lists all the things she should go and see starting with museums:

MOMA

The Brooklyn Museum

The Harlem Museum

The Metropolitan

The Guggenheim

The Whitney

The Frick

The Museum of New York

The Cloisters

The Museum of Holography

The Museum of Photography

The Museum of Broadcasting.

And after he's listed all the museums he runs

through all the nightclubs yuppie gay or underground and follows that with restaurants and finishes with a rapturous account of frogs legs at the Indocine and then he asks whether she's here on holiday or business and offers to give her the grand tour any time and introduces himself as Humphrey Bogart and Marilyn thinks what a wonderfully eloquent statement-maker he is and then he says:

'So what do you do?'

And somewhat reassured by the prospect of talking about herself she gives the usual condensed encapsulated reply:

'Musician journalist writer film-maker model research scientist.'

And Marilyn wonders why no-one ever laughs when she gives the usual condensed encapsulated reply which has nothing much to do with her life or her life history and who would believe that anyone's life would sound like that anyway? but no-one ever says anything and Humphrey the wonderfully eloquent statement-maker Bogart doesn't say anything but just smiles a very nice slightly-bucked-teeth-with-calcium-spots smile from full red rosy lips and a bright red scarf and when he suggests that they go somewhere for a drink or coffee she agrees trying to forget all about her waitressing job and her dilemma about Twentiethcentury and innermost sense of insecurity and anxiety and the fact that she's still hearing voices and can't even remember the jaded world-weary look about Twentiethcentury's face or his beneath-the-appearance dishevelled self.

Outside on the street of freezing winds Marilyn is all of a sudden very very cold and it's as if her ears are going to fall off and the inside of her nose has been sliced with ice as her toes curl up and cramp in her black patent shoes and her 100% cotton socks and then start to ache and go numb and Marilyn mumbles something about the harshness of a northern winter stumbling over yet another pile of stuffed black garbage bags and Humphrey just smiles behind his bright red scarf and tells her and all the very tall shiny buildings that she should buy a scarf and some gloves and some hiking boots and even a hat with ear muffs and that's when Marilyn begins to laugh hysterically and sing folk songs like:

'Kookaburra sits in the old gum tree,' which Humphrey also knows and they both stamp their feet down the street of freezing winds singing and clapping their hands and then finally Humphrey hails a cab and the driver starts talking about the state of the roads as they inch downtown in the rush-hour traffic and Marilyn continues to laugh hysterically until at one stage the driver looks at Humphrey in the mirror and gestures towards Marilyn and says:

'She Ostralian?'

And when Humphrey nods his head and rolls his eyes and sighs with a brisk whisking ejection of breath through his nose the driver starts talking about Crocodile Dundee and they both agree that it's a great film and that it's finally put Ostralia on the map and that Down Under looks like a great place for a vacation and that's when Marilyn stops laughing almost choking and then they start talking about the Brooklyn Bridge.

From the cab it's only a few icy steps to Humphrey's local and once they're inside he orders them two Mexican cocktails and two bowls of gumbo and they sit up at the bar beneath the monitor showing the football and Marilyn begins to defrost and her skin begins to change colour from blue to white to red to pink and Humphrey starts talking about Ostralian films and Paul Hogan and then he asks:

'So what're Ostralian films like?'

And Marilyn says:

'Neo-realist.'

And then Humphrey launches into a jargonised account for and against the death of the author in terms of the birth of the film director and Marilyn listens to Humphrey and isn't really sure what she feels although she knows it's got something to do with sheer stunned and brainless incredulity and amazement and then she experiences an almost hysterical acceleration of her tired and feverish senses as she realises that a lifetime of reading habits have been uninformed and superficial and that she's been brought up on a staple diet of textual closure and common sense which probably means she's bourgeois or middle class or something worse so she says:

'Speaking of criticism one of the first things you notice about this decadent decadent full-of-dead-trees-not-a-breath-of-fresh-air city is—'

And Humphrey interrupts and says:

'But the trees aren't dead they're just—'

But Marilyn ignores him and says:

'Anyway one of the first things you notice is that it's full of film places and film people and it's just like walking into a hundred films at once whether you're in Central Park or a loft in Soho or Battery Park or crossing the Brooklyn Bridge it's all like one long film even people's noses and teeth are post-celluloid which creates this perspective where you actually become one of the characters in a worldwide film script you know? Like this decadent decadent city is the centre of the world and the rest of the world begins here and radiates outwards and living here's like backing a winner where you can see living legends like Dizzy Gillespie live and then watch them die do you know what I mean?'

And Humphrey says:

'Have you ever ridden a subway at about four in the morning when most of the clubs and bars are closed and the cars are full of sleeping people and all these bums lie down across the seats and sleep or just sit there with their heads tilted forwards snoring? because I'd really like to show you my New York the real stuff you know not the tourist traps and all that crap.'

And then she gulps down her third Mexican cocktail and realises that she has to go back to the up-market French restaurant Downtown and that her entire afternoon has been a thinly disguised attempt to avoid her guilty feelings about Liz and her flatmates and to repress her innermost sense of insecurity and anxiety and Marilyn knows with a sense of desolate windswept inevitability that she has to go to work as a waitress even if she's no better than a lousy hack so she leans over and kisses Humphrey the wonderfully eloquent statement-maker Bogart goodbye who says:

'I wonder how long it'll take before you start talking like a Yank?'

And then he asks her to call him up at work when she wants the grand tour and in a moment she's out in her friendly snowy paradise and her body freezes and contracts and crystallises almost shattering and she calls out:

'Taxi,' and nothing happens so she whistles and a cab stops and she gives him the address and later when the cab pulls up she realises that she's three and a half hours late for her first day in her new job in her new life and she's never worked as a waitress before and has no idea what she'll have to do and Liz's sister will probably kill her and as butterflies and Christmas beetles converge on her stomach and crispy cicada shells tap-dance further down her digestive tract she retraces her steps along the black and white tiles up to the pinky-grey expanse of the bar and says:

'Hi.'

And Marilyn tries to listen carefully while Zanuck runs through the specials of the day but she can't hear properly above the persistent nagging voice that keeps pointing the bone and saying:

Chicken—

And:

Hack—

Accusingly so Marilyn has to spend the whole night pretending to be a waitress and makes up her own version of the specials of the day and then drops a piece of cake on her foot near table seven and slops steaming cups of decaff cappuccinos all over their saucers and corks the wine for the deuce near the window and gets all her drink orders wrong and she's just on the way to a table of eight with her second attempt at their drink order of whiskey sours and double-malted scotches on the rocks and one without rocks and dry martinis one with a twist and one with a twist and two pickled onions and a Stoli and tonic in a tall glass when—

Oh my God—

And there's Twentiethcentury Fox with this woman with these God-are-they-silicon? tits which are almost bursting out of her low-cut black backless dress and as soon as Marilyn sees Twentiethcentury she slips on nothing and the tray wobbles and one of the martinis falls over and spills all down the front of one of Liz's flatmate's white silk voile shirt and Marilyn makes a desperate grab to save it that upsets the whole tray and then thinks—

Oh well.

And just lets the whole tray fall and at that moment Marilyn looks at Twentiethcentury and Twentiethcentury looks at Marilyn and his face has this jaded world-weary look about it and he seems deeply dishevelled even in his impeccable does-he-really-work-in-Wall-Street? business suit with the button-down-collar shirt and the striped tie and they stare at each other all chilly and desolate while the tray crashes on the black and white tiled floor and the glass sprays up in a wet and shiny spray and some goes all over Marilyn's shoes and stockings and some falls over near Twentiethcentury's feet and some falls on the woman's low-cut black backless dress and then everything freezes like that for a moment—

Oh Twentiethcentury—

And the next thing Marilyn knows she's back at the bar reordering the drinks while Zanuck cleans up the mess and the table of eight don't mind even when Marilyn still gets the drink order wrong because there's meant to be one dry martini straight up with a cherry and a twist and one Absolute vodka martini on the rocks and two whiskey sours not three and a Stoli-lime-and-soda in a tall glass and one peach margarita and one frozen margarita and one double-malted scotch on the rocks with the water on the side but they still end up leaving fifteen per cent which surprises everyone especially Zanuck.

Much much later that night and early the next morning Marilyn sits hunched over the grimy tiles on her safe settled-beneath-the-cistern seat in Liz's apartment sulking about her wound and pouting about everything that's happened with Twentiethcentury and is still slightly in shock from all the blood and her ride in the ambulance to hospital and she fiddles with the eyeliner pencil in her good hand and she's just about to add the story of how she met Twentiethcentury and why her left hand's in a sling to *The List of Names and Places* when Liz peers in and Marilyn has a lot of trouble forcing herself to meet Liz's eyes but when she does she sees they're full of concern and I-know-just-how-you-feel sisterly understanding so Marilyn smiles weakly but doesn't know what to say when Liz says:

'Too bad about last night huh?' and stares at the walls in grimy tiled silence until Liz says:

'I was thinking that maybe you'd like to go for a winter picnic on the beach at Coney Island?'

And Marilyn says:

'OK.'

And Liz puts her hand on her shoulder and tells her not to worry about losing her job because a friend of hers works in a nightclub and can get her a job any time as a coat check and Marilyn says:

'Thanks,' and abandons the idea of *The List of Names and Places* and puts the eyeliner back in the cupboard and blows her sniffly nose and wipes her soggy eyes on the generic non-brand toilet paper and as soon as Liz leaves Marilyn takes out Twentiethcentury's note and reads:

Marilyn's Almost Terminal New York Adventure

Dear Marilyn,
  Get well soon,
  Twentiethcentury S. Fox Jnr.

And smiles.

When Marilyn finally ventures smilingly out into the lounge room of seemingly secret telephones and hidden light switches where scavenged surplus living sculptures collect dust in the dry churned over-agitated air and—

Atchou—

Sneezes she hears the sporadic bursts of an unidentified electric appliance which sends clouds of hand-blow-dried real potato French fries drifting through the clear blue skies of her mind's eye so she squeezes between the antiquated hissing thumping groaning and gurgling central heating facility and a stack of empty picture frames where she hungrily watches Liz hurl things into an industrial strength cocktail blender.

And Liz says:

'Homemade brandy egg nog want some?' and passes Marilyn a chipped MGM cup of creamy foaming frothy warmth.

And brimming with warm yummy tummy security and enthusiasm Marilyn decides it might just be the right dining time to tell Liz all about Twentiethcentury Fox and Virginia and how she came to be here at all because she's suddenly very calmly sure that she's going to meet Twentiethcentury again and half expecting him to call any second she says:

the potholes are
big enough to
swallow an entire
Toyota Corolla

'How did I ever meet someone like Twentieth-century Fox in a city like this of all places to meet someone like him?

'God.

'But from the moment I first saw him on that TV matinee show it was like we were two people staring at each other from different sides of a windswept street in a chilly desolate wintry cityscape.'

But Liz doesn't hear because of the buzzing whirring of the industrial strength cocktail blender and Marilyn begins to suspect that it's definitely not the right dining time to explain everything to Liz and watches with a:

Why me?

Sigh while Liz pours another jug of creamy foaming frothy warmth into a red checked Warner Bros thermos and says:

'Are you ready?'

And Marilyn adds the chipped MGM cup to the untidy mass of dirty imported tequila sodden glasses and chilli dip smeared Hollywood bowls and the oil soaked floral paper towels which are studded with no longer salty sucked pistachio shells and nods her head absently as Liz brushes past her crying:

'Gloves scarf boots,' just like a check list so Marilyn scrounges around the stack of empty picture frames where she finds a single black leather glove and then she finds an emerald green scarf behind the antiquated hissing thumping groaning gurgling central heating facility which she kicks saying:

'Stupid bloody thing.'

And she can't find any boots and she's just lacing up her black patent shoes when—

Oh oh—

And Liz thrusts her a helmet and bomber jacket and that probably means Marilyn's about to take a ride on a big BMW bike for the first time in her life with a crazy Latino at the handlebars of what is probably a destructively over-powered machine through all those oh-my-god-the-potholes-are-big-enough-to-swallow-an-entire-Toyota-Corolla streets and all the slushy snow traffic and a minus twenty degrees wind-chill factor—

Gulp—

And she finally manages to murmur all lock-jaw lips and sweaty palms something like:

'So where are we going?'

And Liz's voice answers like Darth Vader from somewhere inside her helmet and goggles:

'Macy's.'

And chicken Marilyn watches from a distance while Liz wheels the big black beast from the peach and sage green papered walls of the hallway into the goods lift and twists her scarf nursing her now pounding throbbing wound and thinks reckless last minute I-don't-want-to-do-this-mummy thoughts like:

Dear Twentiethcentury Fox, the only man I almost knew whom I ever truly loved. Goodbye, Marilyn.

And:

Dear Virginia, the deepest friendship I never really expressed but always sensed. Thank you.

But before she can think any more it's-the-end-of-the-world-as-we-know-it thoughts she's following Liz out onto the street where Liz places a helmet over her head and starts up the engine and then pulls Marilyn onto the roaring black beast's back and they join the stampeding herd between a Lincoln Continental and a white stretch limo and suddenly Marilyn's staring into an icy grey blur as Liz speeds down the left lane which should be the slow lane but is really the fast lane and when the hazy outline of another vehicle looms directly in their path Liz starts to drive between lanes until another blurry vehicle pulls out in front of them and Liz shouts:

'Don't lean.'

And Marilyn shouts back between gritty teeth:

'Why not?' as the black beast swerves to one side of a lane and narrowly misses a beaten yellow cab and shudders through a gaping pothole which has Marilyn biting her tongue and chewing her cheeks and begging:

'Please stop please stop,' over and over but to no avail and when everything seems to indicate that they should come to a sudden screeching howling halt Liz runs the red light and dodges the hordes of terror-struck gutter-hugging huddling figures in trench coats glasses scarves and hiking boots of elusive detail and makes a left-hand turn keeping well ahead of the cross-fire traffic and Marilyn lifts her eyes from the road to catch glimpses of dangling giant Christmas baubles all red and green against blurry grey rotting towers and when Liz finally does screech to a halt on the corner of 34th Street and Eighth Avenue Marilyn can barely summon the energy to drag her shuddering leg over the black beast's back and can only nod chatteringly as Liz shoves a small wad of hard currency and a shopping list into her hand and shouts:

'I'll meet you back here in half an hour OK?'

Marilyn is just about to ask where she is when Liz revs up the motor and runs a red light and disappears into the slushy traffic in a blurry grey snow-streaked roar.

And Marilyn struggles to overcome her jelly-kneed paralysis and with a little courageous physiotherapy manages to teach herself to walk again and gets caught up in the milling throng and transported all chattering teeth into the midst of the Macy's New Year cosmetics and jewellery sale where she's momentarily washed ashore in front of a gold-and-diamond-studded watch display and she's just about to say:

Excuse me but could you tell me where the food hall is?

When the gold-toothed black man says:

'Can I help you ma'am?'

And Marilyn thinks:

Ma'am?

And tries to remember what she was going to say but can't and her two floating iceberg eyes drift from his gold-toothed bejewelled face down his gold-tie-pinned emerald green and navy polka dot tie and across his blue and white 100% cotton shirt down to scan the contents of the glittering gold counter where sparkling treasures lie scattered across a shimmering black velvet beach and when his dark hairless hand reaches over the shimmering black velvet and places the silvery gold treasure clattering on the glass top of the counter and he says:

'Simply stunning,' Marilyn just nods her heavy helmet head and chews on her blue lips and then the gold-toothed bejewelled man tilts his flashing gold smile to one side and says:

'You must be Ostralian?'

And he slips her his personally monogrammed card which says:

SIDNEY POITIER

And in a leaning-over-the-counter conspiracy he says:

'Any time you get into any trouble you just give old Sidney a call you hear?'

And Marilyn thinks:

Very handsome.

And that's when her blue lips start moving again and she says:

'Actually I was wondering I mean where's the food hall?'

And Sidney the very handsome Poitier directs her past the perfume counter to the escalator where she contemplates Liz's list:

        Polish sausage
        Piroshki
        Paté
        Pastrami

In one column and:

        Chilli dip
        Corn bread
        Corona

Down the other and Marilyn decides to add:

        Chicken legs

But can't resist the honey roast ribs or the lotus rolls and just about everything else behind the shiny glass counters and ten minutes later Marilyn emerges onto the shivery snowy street with her two rustling plastic bags and even though she can't see the black beast she can hear it roaring from the other side of the coagulated 34th Street and Eighth Avenue crowd:

Liz.

And then Marilyn plunges into the sticky mucus knot of onlookers and separates one membrane from another with seemingly surgical skill until she hears a familiar voice:

'This is my space.'

And then an unfamiliar one:

'This is fucken not your space.'

And then a familiar one:

'I've been driving around in a twenty-mile radius trying to park my fucken bike with you sitting on my ass like some goddamn Jersey trash asshole.'

And then an unfamiliar one:

'I spend half my fucken life looking for a park in this shithole city and this is my goddamn space you dumb fuck.'

And Marilyn peels back the last sticky tissue membrane on one of those please-god-don't-let-this-be-happening-to-me situations and is about to perform surgical closure and flee when Liz screams:

'Hey Marilyn why don't you tell this Jersey trash asshole whose fucken space this is?'

And that's when Marilyn lays eyes on the beast in all its traffic-stopping roaring glory and a black denim white Reeboks red ear-muffed form thumps the bonnet of his shit green TransAm and shouts:

'Frankie Baby Sinatra don't take shit from nobody,' between his frothing lips and Marilyn rises to the please-God-don't-let-this-be-happening-to-me situation and places the helmet on her head and packs her rustling bags under the seat and then she addresses the congealed bespeckled gutter-hugging crowd with:

'Excuse me but can anyone please tell us how to get to the Museum of Broadcasting we don't want to miss the Jackie Gleeson retrospective?'

And Frankie Baby Sinatra turns and stares stunned

into silence and Liz smiles a very wide all-right-sister smile and the crowd murmurs all-right-sister:

'Oh yeah.'

And:

'Ooh-ee.'

And then a man wearing a Prince of Wales check cashmere scarf and horn rimmed light sensitive tinted glasses and a navy blue double breasted trench coat and black Timberland galoshes steps forward and says:

'Are you Ostralian?'

And flashes his personally monogrammed business card and the crowd holds its breath and wonders and Marilyn's just about to say:

You must be a film producer—

When the man seems to stumble and slide on the icy slush and that's when Liz comes back to life and leaps on the bike and says:

'Hold on,' as they lurch forwards with a mighty roar and the crowd cheers and sings:

> *Waltzing Matilda, waltzing Matilda*
> *You'll come a-waltzing Matilda with me*
> *And—*

And soon everything is a stinging grey blur as Liz speeds off between the lanes and shouts:

'Don't lean.'

And Marilyn just closes her eyes and holds on tight and lets go of her mind until the beast finally shudders to a halt outside the security doors of Liz's apartment block and in the lift Liz complains about:

'Shit green TransAms.'

And:

'Jersey trash assholes.'

And how they should:

'Raise the toll for the Holland Street Tunnel.'

And when Marilyn says nothing Liz sneaks a peak at her strange silent guest and watches as Marilyn strokes her wound in a series of delicate caresses to her protruding pink fingertips while her smudgy blue eyes stare moistly past the peach and sage green papered walls of the hallway and her blue lips move silently beneath her deeply furrowed brow and Liz wonders about Marilyn and Twentiethcentury and where she comes from and where she's going to and what she thinks about and how she feels after being assaulted on her first night in her new job in her new life but she doesn't ask and soon turns her attention to the front door where she jiggles jaggles twists and rattles the middle most antiquated of the three tarnished brass deadlocks until suddenly:

Holy fuck.

And the key becomes very stuck and refuses to budge and they're out of luck and the whole deal sucks shit:

Aaargh.

Liz doesn't take this very well at all because she's suffering from various nervous disorders somewhat inappropriately associated with PMTs which in this case have more to do with CODs and the situation induces a fairly hostile frenzied response which is also creatively verbose and characteristically violent and Marilyn—

Gulp—

Suddenly finds herself confronted by a scene of moderate broken fingernails destruction with lots of

139

flaking paint and scraps of metal and random piles of plaster and indented karate kick footprints in doors and walls and somewhere in the middle of all this Marilyn hears a muffled sobbing whining and senses that it might be the right post-breakdown time to tell Liz her how-she-came-to-be-here-anyway story so she sits down next to Liz's shuddering huddled form and says:

'I know you're wondering about my mysterious missing friends and why I turned up on your doorstep all lost alone and confused and I think you should know all about Twentiethcentury Fox and what happened last night.'

And Marilyn pauses to see if Liz's listening and she wipes some of Liz's dyed natural frizzy hair out of her smudged-mascara eyes and mops a bit of the fairly hostile frenzied response perspiration from her smooth shiny brow and as Liz's sobbing whining gradually subsides Marilyn tells her all about Twentiethcentury and what happened last night although Liz doesn't listen from the beginning because she's lost deep down in a subterranean primordial pit of primal pain which feels a bit like:

Fucken asshole mother fucking son of a—

And the first words Liz does hear are:

'Anyway Liz I reckon I owe you my life.'

Although they aren't the first words Marilyn says because the first words are:

'You see Liz it all starts when I see one of his historic TV appearances on a matinee show which I can't stop myself from watching despite my allergy and all the undesirable side effects and the whole thing seems to have this certain desolate windswept inevitability about it because it's a rainy New Year's Day and I'm suffering from a bout of desperate soul searching depression and tears stream down my face because of the TV as I stare deeply into his eyes and then I notice his beneath-the-appearance dishevelled self and the jaded world-weary look about his face and I don't notice his brown eyes or brown hair or the colour of his striped tie or the shape of his hands or what colour his skin is or any of the details of his impeccable does-he-really-work-in-Wall-Street? business suit.

'And the host of the talk show looks interested and impressed by everything Twentiethcentury Fox says and I'm intrigued and fascinated because I know he's talking about money although it sounds like he's really talking about the buying and selling of things like seats and these seats may or may not be on the floor and then he tells us the story of how he started with one seat which was an independent seat and how he worked every day from this seat on the floor of the main room until he sold that seat for a lot of money and then he didn't work on the floor of the main room for a few years and then the whole place crashed and the lives of thousands of people were shattered into a million tiny pieces and so he bought a lot more seats on the floor for almost nothing with the money he got from selling the first seat in the main room and some of the new seats were in the main room but others were in the garage and others were in the new blue room but somehow these seats don't really exist and no-one ever sits on them but without one you can't work as an indepen-dent on any of the floors and it's all very abstract and I've never been able to work out how you can make all that money from nothing and the way money seems to be able to appear out of nothing at all and then during the interview they flash his name up on the screen and it says:

'*Twentiethcentury S. Fox Jnr.*

'And I take out my pen and write it down on some newspaper and fold it away and then I stare blankly at the commercials stunned and brainless and it's just after that that I make the first phone call to you because International Directory Assistance makes a mistake but at the time I don't realise this so you see I think you're Twentiethcentury's housekeeper and I keep ringing and you keep taking messages which of course Twentieth-century never gets and I just keep ringing you back remember? Because at this stage I know that I have to speak to Twentiethcentury and from there it isn't long before I know that I have to see Twentiethcentury so I decide to come here and then you find me the job working as the illegal alien waitress in the up-market French restaurant Downtown where I eventually do meet Twentiethcentury Fox as I knew I would.'

And that's when Liz begins to surface from the sub-terranean primordial pit and to let go of all her sub-limely intense indescribable pain and things begin to slide into perspective and she realises that even if it does cost a couple of hundred Cash On Delivery dollars for a locksmith and new lock well then she'll just have to find the money somehow and then it occurs to her that her strange no-longer-silent guest may have some money and maybe Marilyn will pay for a locksmith and that's when she hears Marilyn say:

'Anyway Liz I reckon I owe you my life.'

So Liz interrupts in a drained husky voice:

'A couple of hundred dollars will do.'

Although Marilyn doesn't hear because she's already started to tell the bit about the restaurant:

'Anyway so I turn up to work and I'm really only a hack pretending to be a waitress and I make up my own version of the specials of the day and then I drop a piece of cake on my foot near table seven and slop steaming cups of decaff cappuccinos all over their saucers and cork the wine for the deuce near the window and get all my drink orders wrong and I'm just on my way to a table of eight with my second attempt at their drink order I mean I was so bad and then suddenly—

'*Oh my God*—

'There's Twentiethcentury Fox with this woman with these God-are-they-silicon? tits which are almost bursting out of her low-cut black backless dress and as soon as I see Twentiethcentury I slip on nothing and the tray wobbles and one of the martinis falls over and spills and I make a desperate grab to save it that upsets the whole tray and then I think—

'*Oh well*—

'And just let the whole tray fall and at that moment I look at Twentiethcentury and Twentiethcentury looks at me and his face has this jaded world-weary look about it and he seems deeply dishevelled even in his impeccable does-he-really-work-in-Wall-Street? business suit with the button-down-collar shirt and the striped tie and we stare at each other all chilly and desolate while the tray crashes on the black and white tiled floor and the glass sprays up in a wet and shiny sea spray and some goes all over my shoes and stockings and some falls over near Twentiethcentury's feet and some falls on the woman's low-cut black backless dress and then everything freezes like that for a moment.'

And Marilyn pauses for effect and looks meaningfully

at Liz who nods and says:

'So that's why you got the sack.'

And Marilyn takes a deep breath and says:

'No there's more,' and stands up and brings out the winter picnic plastic bags and they spread the tightly wrapped packages out on the rustling plastic bags and Liz unwraps a very large package and says:

'Assorted sushi was that on the list?'

And then swallows one whole and says through brimming lips:

'Mmm these taste good,' and reaches over and opens another smaller package:

'Deep fried honey chicken legs oh yeah! Did you get any sweet chilli plum sauce?'

And Marilyn shakes her head while Liz wades into the next package and then Marilyn stands up again and paces up and down and throws her arms around as she says:

'Anyway then I have to go up to Twentiethcentury's table and to start with I get all the specials wrong and he just keeps on looking at me as I go on to cork the wine and forget the bread and put the salad dressing straight onto the salad instead of serving it on the side and I can't look at the woman because those God-are-they-silicon? tits make me nervous and I can't take my eyes off Twentiethcentury and we seem to stare at each other from different sides of a windswept street in a chilly desolate wintry cityscape for hours and the woman keeps clearing her throat or tapping the table with her fork and I finally top it all off by serving the woman's roast pheasant in the rich boozy sauce and I say to her as I place the hot plate on the table:

'"Madam here we have your roast silicons in the

rich boozy sauce."

'And as I say this Twentiethcentury looks at me and I look at him and we start laughing and I'm still holding Twentiethcentury's grilled lemon sole and as I laugh the plate goes slightly off balance and Twentieth-century and I both see it slowly slide down the back of the woman's low-cut black backless dress and I can't stop laughing and I almost black out and have to hold onto the edge of the table and that's when I notice that I'm hardly breathing and I taste this dry blood taste in the back of my throat and my knees are just like jelly and then I hear this far-off scream that must be the woman as I slowly slide into blackness and then I feel this jabbing pain in my hand which makes me open my eyes as the fork penetrates the skin through the back of my hand that's still holding white-knuckled onto the table and then I watch as the woman pulls the fork out and then plunges it back in and then the blood begins to spurt out in neat red streams and then I fall back and drop down into wads of cottonwool and that's when I must pull the table down on top of me as I pass out.'

And Liz belches softly and says:

'So that's what happened to your hand would you like some of these honey roast ribs? They're delicious.'

And Marilyn shakes her head:

'No thanks.'

And meanwhile the movie star from the penthouse upstairs is watching and listening from his hiding place on the peach and sage green papered landing unable to resist the sheer animal magnetism of that Ossie accent and keeps peeping down admiringly at Marilyn's captivating presence and her hypnotically hyper performance and wonders about the disaster-struck doorstep and the semi-masticated remains and even though there are a thousand things he should be doing he can't seem to tear himself away from this extremely-attractive-in-a-blonde-haired-blue-eyed-big-busted-way woman:

Very Marilyn-with-a-touch-of-Meryl.

And keeps wondering whether the Twentieth-century Fox she's talking about is THE Twentieth-century Fox because it sounds like it is but how could it be and:

What's wrong with her arm?

And he can't decide whether he should go down and offer to help them with their door or just keep listening and:

Isn't she that Off Off Broadway hopeful who works the bookstalls off Central Park?

But just then the woman starts talking again in that Ossie accent so he stays sitting cross-legged on the landing and closes his eyes.

And meanwhile Liz's picking at the semi-masticated remains and feeling vaguely nauseous and thinking:

And like I know I'm not fat but I mean I've still got to watch what I eat because you know one day I might get fat and then maybe I'll lose control and then never be able to lose it again and wow what a pig-out I mean like I feel really bad and I'm not going to eat anything fattening for a few days now but those honey roast ribs are delicious and I might just have one more but that's it and no more hand-blow-dried real potato French fries or brandy egg nog for breakfast uh uhh.

And Marilyn thinks Liz's concentrated silence is an indication for her to start talking again having no idea about Liz's food obsession which is very different to Twentiethcentury Fox's food obsession because Liz is predominantly worried about her thighs and her waistline whereas Twentiethcentury Fox is mostly concerned with the functioning of his digestive tract and the condition of his shit whereas Marilyn's digestive tract is more like an extension of her other sensory organs with its tap dancing cicada shells and Christmas beetles and anyway Marilyn finishes the story about Twentiethcentury and her wound:

'And then Twentiethcentury leaps to his feet and then the woman starts to scream and then the manager comes over and starts screaming and Twentiethcentury slaps the woman to stop her from screaming and then she starts to cry hot little-girl tears and then someone calls an ambulance and meanwhile I'm dreaming about working in a restaurant as a hack waitress only I can't serve anyone because my hands are full of these little white bags of drugs that I'm trying to hide but I can't find anywhere to hide them and the manager keeps following me and I keep dodging him and when I wake up the first thing I see are two dozen long-stemmed red roses and I think:

'*Oh no I'm dead*.

'And I have this dry blood taste in the back of my throat and my head's pounding blood through the courses of my brain and my hand feels numb and just then I see a note in the roses that has *Marilyn—the waitress* written on it so I close my eyes and fall asleep in a land of no dreams and when I wake up I ask the nurse to open the note and she does so I read it and this is what it says: *Dear Marilyn, Get well soon, Twentiethcentury S. Fox Jnr.*'

147

and then Liz opens one of the bottles of Corona with an attachment on her BMW key ring and passes it to Marilyn:

'So you came all this way because of some Wall Street type on a TV matinee show thinking I was his housekeeper or something—did you try any of the lotus rolls?'

And Marilyn just sighs and shakes her head and says:

'Should we call the caretaker about the door?'

And Liz takes a swig from her bottle and says:

'Well you see the super's on his yearly vacation and that's why I'm so pissed because this means we're talking about locksmiths and CODs and like I was wondering if you . . . I was wondering if you could just tide me over because I haven't been getting much work lately and at this stage of my career I should be thinking Off Off Broadway not off Central Park and the bookstalls you know what I mean and like I was wondering if you could lend me a couple of hundred dollars you know for the door?'

And Marilyn is just about to answer when Liz bursts in with:

'Do you guys have dollars in Ostralia like do

one of the best

views of the

Chrysler Building

this city has

to offer

you have Ostralian dollars?'

Before Marilyn has a chance to answer the first question so when Marilyn says:

'Yes but—'

Liz leaps up and squeals all piggy-pink enthusiasm and hugs and kisses her and says a lot of emotionally over-wrought things which leaves Marilyn all lockjawed and breathless and ultimately ineffectual when it comes to stopping Liz from disappearing down the nine flights of stairs into the cold and shiveringly grim afternoon in search of a locksmith:

Oh shit.

And Marilyn moans and groans and curses Virginia and her too-enigmatic deeper self and it's all Virginia's fault anyway and she wouldn't be in this situation if Virginia had appeared at the airport because now she'd be staying with Virginia in a hotel instead of with Liz and her colony of frozen cockroaches and:

God Virginia.

But then if she hadn't met Liz and learnt how to dance with Cary she wouldn't have met Twentiethcentury last night at the restaurant:

Oh Twentiethcentury.

But then she's sure that she would have met him anyway even without Liz's help and maybe if she'd met him in different circumstances things would've turned out differently because she probably would have met him on the subway like R. what-the-fuck-does-the-R.-stand-for? Hudson or in a museum like Humphrey the won-derfully eloquent statement-maker Bogart and instead of having a dozen roses in a dented Quakers Oats tin on top of one of the amplifiers in Liz's apartment and one arm in a sling she'd have a personally monogrammed card with a phone number or a lunch date or a dinner date or maybe she'd be spending her afternoon with Twentiethcentury right now in a quiet bar instead of sitting on a disaster-struck doorstep surrounded by Macy's bags and the semi-masticated remains of the winter picnic at Coney Island and Marilyn almost rushes straight out to the nearest subway station or museum to meet Twentiethcentury:

Oh Twentiethcentury.

But then:

Oh no.

And:

I've probably blown it with Twentiethcentury anyway.

And that's when Marilyn surrenders to a sweeping tide of self-pity and guilt-related emotions and bursts into stormy tears all thunder and lightning and then she slides down the wall all quivering whimpering gasps.

And when the rivers of her precious bodily fluids finally run dry she begins to pack away the winter picnic at Coney Island lunch all sniffling I-want-to-go-home-now soggy-sleeved sorrow and that's when she hears someone say in a deep tender voice:

'Anything I can do to help?'

And Marilyn just shakes her head and wipes her nose on her soggy sleeve and breathes deep jerky breaths all shuddering shoulders and rustles the Macy's bags protectively trying not to imagine what she must look like and thinking lots of leave-me-alone thoughts but the man doesn't leave her alone and sits down next to her on the disaster-struck doorstep and looks at Liz's bike and says:

'That's a beautiful piece of machinery you have there.'

151

And when Marilyn turns her smeary smudged bleary blue eyes towards this well-meaning neighbour the first thing she notices is that he's not wearing any of the things all the other men she's met so far have been wearing like trench coats and hiking boots because this man's wearing a fluffy white terry towelling bathrobe and a pair of coffee coloured genuine leather moccasins and from what Marilyn can see in her first post-breakdown tear-stained glance this is also absolutely all he appears to be wearing which seems a little unusual if not completely bizarre and when Marilyn's quite sure that she's not going to burst into tears again she lets her eyes drift wearily to his face and if Marilyn was the type of person to faint in times of crisis or suffer incontinency during outbursts of hysteria it's highly probable that Marilyn would certainly have fainted or defecated or done something suitably dramatic because when she looks into the intense brown eyes beneath the heavy brows and the receding ruffled curls above the dark stubble and sensual lips she recognises one of those instantly familiar ageless Hollywood faces of elusive identity but unmistakable stature one of those oh-my-God-that's . . . that's . . . who-*is*-that? faces with the crowd-stopping smile and the understated sense of nineties cool and reserved charm and Marilyn begins to taste a dry blood taste in the back of her throat and thinks:

Who is this? Oh my God oh fuck what's his name? What's his name?

And then the movie star says:

'Is this your key?'

And passes Marilyn one of Liz's bent tarnished brass keys and then says predictably from his dazzling array of incisors:

152

'You must be Ostralian?'

And then he nods his head slowly and says:

'What you need for those locks is a little oil to loosen them up because they're probably just a little stiff you see they'd be pretty old and probably went in with the building like these apartment buildings went up in the twenties or thirties and a lot of the apartments still have the old fixtures like the old locks and the old plumbing and the original central heating systems that make all the hissing thumping and gurgling sounds like you know the ones? And all of these original fixtures are just great except that you need to keep chasing the super for every little thing and that's why I had my penthouse upstairs renovated because I couldn't stand the constant battles with the locks and the blocked sinks and I had a couple of the other apartments in the building renovated as well and now a lot of people are thinking of selling out to a big developer who's prepared to pay top dollar and there's only a few of us left who are still trying to fight the developer through the Co-Operative Board because there's a good chance that they'll buy the block next door which is a rental and then they'll build another one of those goddamn awful towers but anyway why don't you come upstairs while I find some spray to fix these locks and something to straighten out the keys and meanwhile you can enjoy one of the best views of the Chrysler Building this city has to offer OK so are you an actress?'

And Marilyn gives him the usual condensed encapsulated reply:

'Musician journalist writer film-maker model research scientist.'

And the movie star says:

'Oh really how interesting,' and raises his heavy brow and Marilyn stands up on cramped shaky legs and gathers the Macy's bags and the movie star picks up the keys all white hairy legs and tight calf muscles and Marilyn follows him up the stairs thinking:

Very Mickey-Rourke-with-a-touch-of-Dustin-Hoffman I mean this never would've happened back home and I wonder if he's the guy who's just recently gone into directing or was it politics?

And when Marilyn steps over the polished marble doorstep into the breathtaking open plan sophisticated kitsch loft-style penthouse she doesn't notice all the tiny columns archways and lattice on the patio or the dazling array of hand-crafted silk Moroccan and Persian rugs or the gleaming parquet or the eclectic bricolage or the photographs of the movie star's property near Toronto because she's instantly transfixed by the decorative spire of the Chrysler Building which is framed between two rotting towers and she stands at the full-length tinted glass sliding doors with her nose to the glass and her Macy's bag to her chest and meanwhile the movie star disappears into a walk-in pantry and rummages around for some oil and a hammer and when he emerges he finds Marilyn stretched out on one of his silk rugs staring dreamily out the window and he calls from the doorway:

'Help yourself to the icebox I'll be right back.'

And while Marilyn lies mesmerised by the decorative spire of the Chrysler Building she hopes cross-your-fingers that the movie star will be able to open the door to Liz's apartment so that they won't have to pay for a locksmith and then Marilyn won't have to tell Liz that she hasn't got any money left or that she came to Manhattan with less than $100 Australian to find the love of her life who she'd never even met which does sound a little crazy even if she did know with a certain sense of desolate windswept inevitability that she would meet Twentieth-century eventually and even worse than this Marilyn doesn't want to think about what Twentiethcentury must think of her and how she's probably fucked up her one big chance to meet him which means that everything's lost and there isn't even any point in trying her luck with Directory Assistance because Twentiethcentury probably doesn't even want to know about her and probably only sent her the note and the dozen long-stemmed reds out of embarrassment and pity and all she wants to do now is to go home.

And this is why Marilyn decides to ring up Qantas to book a return ticket to Sydney ASAP but it takes a long time to find the phone which is so grey and flat that it's almost invisible and when she finally does get through a woman's voice says that the first available seat is in six months' time which makes Marilyn think that Paul Hogan has done a lot more for Australia than anyone realises so Marilyn spells out her name three times and the woman places her at the end of a long long waiting list and when Marilyn hangs up the phone she's already forgotten all about Liz and the locksmith and Twentiethcentury and Virginia because now all she can think about is going home:

I want to go home now mummy.

And the movie star passes her a drink in a square frosted glass as if he'd never left and Marilyn tries to take a sip from a straight edge but it dribbles all down her chin and the movie star laughs and Marilyn laughs and he shows her how to drink from the corner of the square frosted glass and offers her a seat on a little three-legged NASA-designed stool but Marilyn prefers the rugs so they lie down and watch the lights come on in the Chrysler Building and Marilyn's sure she can hear bells ringing and the movie star starts to talk about his childhood and how he was destined to be an actor from a very early age and after a while he asks Marilyn lots of questions about Ostralia that all seem to have something to do with sharks and crocodiles and melanoma so Marilyn tells him all about poisonous snakes and spiders and the blue-ringed octopus and the Portuguese man-of-war and the ozone and the movie star says he thinks it sounds like a great place for a vacation which makes Marilyn laugh and then he laughs and they both roll around on the rugs laughing and then he says:

'Have you ever been ice-skating?'

And Marilyn says:

'No.'

And then he says:

'I'd love to take you ice-skating and then maybe we could grab a bite to eat.'

And Marilyn says:

'Well my arm.'

And he says:

'Do you want to see my gyroscope?'

And Marilyn says:

'What about ice-skating?'

And he says:

'I've got a bottle of Louis Roederer on ice.'

And turns on the crowd-stopping smile and the understated sense of eighties cool and reserved charm and Marilyn says:

'OK.'

But suddenly it's not OK it's much more like:

What the fuck?

Because a pounding wave of dance music breaks through the security grille and washes all over the dazzling array of hand-crafted silk Moroccan and Persian rugs and the gleaming parquet floor and the eclectic bricolage and the photographs of the movie star's property near Toronto and all over Marilyn and the movie star and out onto the patio and breaks the spell of the Chrysler Building and the lights and all the rolling around laughing on the rugs and seriously undermines the otherwise irresistible effects of the movie star's crowd-stopping smile and his understated sense of nineties cool and his reserved charm and Marilyn remembers about Liz and the locksmith and stands up and the movie star stands up and they laugh and the movie star shrugs and Marilyn smiles and leans over and yells in his ear:

'I'll meet you downstairs.'

And the movie star nods and Marilyn lets herself out through the polished marble doorstep and closes the security grille with an oh-my-God-whoever-you-are-you're-very-very-nice slam and the music gets louder and louder and when she reaches Liz's apartment she's confronted by a tidal wall of sound and people spill out of the disaster-struck doorway onto the landing still wearing black hats and ear muffs and gloves and scarves and full-length tattered grey or black overcoats from outside and Marilyn wonders why no-one told her about the party and walks up to a tall thin girl wearing black and white striped socks and Dr Marten's boots and says:

'Have you seen Liz?'

And the girl leans over and slurs behind Ray Bans:

'Liz who?'

And Marilyn just shrugs and squeezes between the girl and a guy wearing shredded black leather pants and a ripped white T-shirt and a black leather bomber jacket covered with black satin bows and safety pins and a black leather cap and Marilyn smiles:

'Hi.'

And then he leans over smiling:

'Hi how are you?' as a gold pyramid earring dangles and jangles and he squeezes her shoulder and says:

'Hey are you Ostralian?'

And Marilyn says:

'Is Liz here?'

And a guy dressed up like a witch doctor with a stethoscope around his neck tweaks her nipple and says:

'Hey I just love your costume.'

And Marilyn smiles:

'Hmm,' and nurses her wound while the guy with the earring says:

'I'm Malcolm and this is X the Witch Doctor and we both play in an underground reggae band and we're playing tonight at a club in Brooklyn out on Flatbush and Liz's going to meet you there so you might as well come with us.'

And then they leave and out on the street Malcolm points to his car and says:

'See this this is a brand new car man and it's already covered in shit I mean look at all this crap fuck man like one day in this shithole city and I've already got myself an $8000 heap of shit.'

And X the Witch Doctor climbs into the back with his orange and purple zigzag medicine bag on his lap and Marilyn sits in the front and Malcolm puts on a tape and X the Witch Doctor says:

'Why don't we just stop at the car wash on Flatbush?'

And Malcolm says as the tape rewinds:

'We ain't got time man.'

And X the Witch Doctor says:

'Sure we got time they'll wait.'

And the car lurches forward into the inching red caterpillar tail-lights line and then the tape starts and it's so loud Marilyn has to open the window and everywhere Marilyn looks there are clusters of moon-faces staring at Malcolm's $8000 heap of shit and then X the Witch Doctor taps her on the shoulder and passes her a big fat crackling joint and Marilyn takes a long hard drag and then passes the joint to Malcolm and leans back and thinks:

This is nice this is really nice just waves of sound and everything's spinning round and if I just hold onto the seat everything's going to be all right yeah this is really nice.

And Marilyn slides into a buzzing honeyed place of no dreams and her arm slips painlessly out of her sling and she only opens her eyes when the car screeches to a halt outside the car wash on Flatbush Avenue where Malcolm passes her another big fat crackling joint and Marilyn takes a few more long hard drags—

Cough cough—

And then the car inches forward on little pitter-pat feet and furry tentacles lash out at the windscreen and the arms swirl and swish and then it's raining and everything's black rubber and Marilyn starts laughing and Malcolm starts laughing and turns the windscreen wipers on and soon they're all collapsed and gasping and coughing and Marilyn can't stop crying and the tape ends suddenly and clicks off and everyone stops laughing and then Malcolm pays the money and they speed off skidding on the icy wrong side of the road and then they drive up into a dark lonely petrol station and park the car and Malcolm turns off the engine and Marilyn is suddenly very scared in the dark quiet creaking doors petrol station in Brooklyn with Malcolm and X the Witch Doctor.

Help.

And when she opens the door she breathes deeply and slowly and braces herself to run just in case and she slams the door and turns to the road and takes two jerky steps and then slides on the ice and lands flat as a pancake and Malcolm laughs and she can't breathe and then they each take a hand and pull her up and then Malcolm hands her a heavy bag of leads and they stumble up a red stairway behind the petrol station and Marilyn almost leaps with joy when she sees all the other people and soon she's smiling and sort of dancing and bobbing her head and she laughs a bit to herself and then she sees Liz and they both scream and run and soon she's wrapped in Liz's arms and smothered in heady frangipani and Liz grabs her and drags her to the dance floor and soon Marilyn's dancing and shaking and gyrating and spinning and she can't stop and one song becomes another and another and finally Liz shouts in her ear:

'Let's go to the bathroom.'

And in the bathroom they swig brandy from Liz's

hip flask and Liz says:

'We got evicted today.'

And Marilyn says:

'Oh no.'

And Liz shrugs and swigs and says:

'They've given us two weeks.'

And Marilyn shakes her head and Liz says:

'Yeah,' and swigs and then:

'As soon as the band's finished let's get Malcolm to take us to this great club in Alphabet City you'll love it like it only opens at four.'

So later on they leave in Malcolm's shiny car all skidding and slushy on the icy white wrong side of the road to Manhattan.

malcolm and Liz and Marilyn pull up in a back lane in Alphabet City all blaring music and jokes about Ostralian slang:

'Fuck a chicken—'

And:

'Cool as a cucumber.'

Malcolm passes around some white powdered drugs and they all snort and sniffle and try not to sneeze and swallow globs down the backs of their throats—

Yuck—

And while Marilyn and Malcolm lean against a pole and breathe fast and let their eyes get caught by everything that moves and swallow and hold their noses and sniff deep scratchy sniffs Liz goes up to the fabulously nail-biting Door to talk their way in and motormouth Marilyn says:

'I hope we get in.'

And Malcolm coughs back in a deep drippy voice:

'Yeah this place is really fantastic it's like the most happening club in New York I mean it only opens at four in the morning you see the girl on the Door she's new and real unpredictable and like she's a friend of a friend of mine's brother's girlfriend and man she's meant to be some tough chick like a real pain in the ass you know?'

the icy white
wrong side of
the road to
Manhattan

And then Liz smiles over:

'It's lucky none of us have blue Afros.'

And they all laugh and wrap their arms around each other's shoulders and then Malcolm hands over the $30 to the fabulously nail-biting Door who nods and—

Phhit—

Spits out a bit of nail all sneering and upturned nose and they all worm inside and Liz whispers:

'Filing's right out this week like nail-biting's back with a vengeance did you see whether she was wearing any polish I forgot to look I was so nervous.'

And takes a few tentative bites at her smooth long black nails.

Meanwhile Marilyn's eyes leapfrog around in the strange blue light and the music almost knocks her over in light-headed confusion and her feet feel like spongy springs and her knees seem really loose and she leans over and shouts in Liz's ear:

'I didn't know you had punks here too.'

And their eyes get stuck to faces as they flash past in all the fluoro pink and black and white phosphorescent skin and somehow they can't find Malcolm and Marilyn's tongue whirligigs around her lips and her eyes dart wildly and then she catches sticky sight of a bright red scarf and a navy double-breasted trench coat in the middle of all the fluoro pink and black and white phosphorescent skin so she grabs Liz and they wriggle through a tight cluster of Grateful Dead T-shirts and whole Amazon forests of amazing hair and earrings and Humphrey the wonderfully eloquent statement-maker Bogart turns around and smiles an even nicer slightly-bucked-teeth-with-calcium-spots smile and says:

'I see you found the real New York without me.'

And wraps an arm around her shoulders and hugs her tight and tells his friends:

'This is a great friend of mine Marilyn from Ostralia Marilyn I'd like you to meet Harpo and Groucho.'

And meanwhile Marilyn's smiling a wide coked-up this-is-really-great smile and her jaws jerk and clamp and chew her cheeks and she shouts in Humphrey's ear:

'This place is really great it's really strange it's really crazy it's really amazing.'

And Humphrey the wonderfully eloquent statement-maker Bogart yells back:

'Yeah.'

And Marilyn's tongue whirligigs again and her motormouth grinds into gear and she shouts:

'It's amazing that you're here.'

And Humphrey yells back:

'Yeah,' through his very nice slightly-bucked-teeth-with-calcium-spots smile but his wonderfully eloquent:

'Can I buy you a drink?' is too late because Liz's already dragged Marilyn away through the eye-catching soul-snatching labyrinth to the stairs where they join the grinding queue to the bathroom.

And Marilyn twitches and turns in I-can't-stand-still exasperation and her head zaps and zooms and snaps on her neck as she jerks searchingly from one face to another and she begins to taste a dry blood taste in the back of her throat and submits—

Oh Twentiethcentury—

To the bluey green explosion of stars as galaxies collide and that's when Twentiethcentury's face

165

appears before her in a circle of shining white light.

And Marilyn grabs with greedy grasping hands at his beneath-the-appearance-dishevelled self and the jaded world-weary look about his face but—

Bloody hell—

His face keeps floating away and dissolving and melting and then a shadow passes over the circle of shining white light and everything starts spinning all black and down down down down and spinning and dark and down and Liz nudges her:

'How is it for you?'

And Marilyn nods:

'Great really great,' and wraps her arm around Liz's shoulder and breathes deep breaths and tries not to sink down all shaky knees and grinding teeth.

And then they both start talking to a so-are-you-into-film-or-video? guy in a tuxedo who's next in the queue and words like:

'. . . film . . .'

'. . . video . . .'

'. . . video . . .'

'. . . film . . .'

'. . . Marilyn . . .'

'. . . Liz . . .'

'. . . Lawford . . .'

'. . . hi . . .'

Fly around all restless and free and giggles and then:

'So.'

And after what seems like an eon or an age of floating phrases and shiny smiles the guy from LA starts tugging at his bow tie all trembling fingers and shiny sweat and bashes on the door:

'Hurry up in there for Christsakes.'

166

And then he mumbles something about repression and his therapist called Grace Kelly and shouts:

'Some junkie's probably OD'd in there,' and starts kicking the door.

Liz and Marilyn whisper:

'Oh oh.'

'He's crazy.'

'A fruitcake.'

'He's freaking me out.'

'Me too.'

And hold hands in the dark and roll their eyes and stand back all frightened and jangling nerves.

And then—

Crash—

The door crashes open all splintering shuddering and—

Oh my God oh my God oh my GOD—

It's Twentiethcentury Fox and Marilyn looks at Twentiethcentury and Twentiethcentury looks at Marilyn and it's just like Marilyn and Twentiethcentury are two people staring at each other from different sides of a windswept street in a chilly desolate wintry cityscape and all of a sudden everything's:

Oh Twentiethcentury—

And:

Oh Marilyn—

Even though Twentiethcentury's slumped on the can with a notepad and a pencil all dishevelled and world-weary and jaded and sweaty with his pants around his ankles.

But then—

Oh oh—

And that's when the guy from LA blows his fuse

167

and cracks up and starts screaming abuse all wired up strung out fucked up and freaked out.

Meanwhile all Marilyn can hear is the surging swelling incoming tide of a heavenly choir which is singing:

> Hallelujah
> Hallelujah
> Hallelujah hallelujah hallelujah

And the timpani are beating wildly and the strings are soaring sweetly shrill and then the clouds part to let the sun beam down all golden and warm and wonderful.

But then—

Bang crash pow—

The guy from LA goes berserk and throws Twentieth-century down the narrow winding stairs:

'You fuckwit.'

That's when Marilyn:

> Faster than a speeding bullet
> More powerful than a locomotive
> Able to leap tall buildings in a single
> bound . . .

Tears the bandages from her wrist and spontaneously summons one of those summer nights at the Police Citizens Boys Club karate kicks and—

Hai ya—

Sends the fuckwit in a tux crashing down after Twentiethcentury on the narrow winding stairs and Liz screams and a skinhead grabs Marilyn's arms and pins them behind her back and Marilyn sobs:

'Twentiethcentury.'

And Liz says:

'Let her go you creep.'

But the skinhead doesn't let her go so Liz kicks the skinhead in the shins with each of her shiny black pointed patent stilettos and the skin squeals all fiery shins and collapses moaning:

'Fucken asshole Ostralians.'

And Marilyn bounds forwards all chilly and desolate and Hallelujah to meet Twentiethcentury as he staggers up the stairs pulling his trousers up as he comes with his tie askew and his shirt unbuttoned and his does-he-really-work-in-Wall-Street? jacket slung over his left shoulder and his face is all shiny and wet and his lips seem too big and too red and too soft and then:

Oh Twentiethcentury.

And Twentiethcentury wobbles straight over to Marilyn and leans his head on her shoulder and whines:

'Oh man I've been looking for you for hours and hours like I've been to every club every fucken bar just looking for you and huh I mean here you are like man I can't believe you're finally here to take me home I mean like my brain's beginning to rattle in my skull and my head's pounding and my neck's real tight and I could do with a little massage and I've got indigestion or monosodium glutamate poisoning or something from some take-out crap I had earlier on and I was in a car crash in a cab and I hit my head man I got a fucken bump the size of an egg right here see? and when I fell down the stairs just then I bruised my arm and I think I put my back out.'

And Marilyn brushes stray locks from his hot

sweaty forehead and strokes the thick hair at the base of his neck and thinks —

Poor baby —

And rolls her eyes at Liz who smiles and winks and Twentiethcentury moans:

'Oh yeah yeah that's nice oh just there yeah that's it that's nice soft oh,' and twists his head and cracks his neck and hunches his shoulders and then lets his arms flop loose at his sides and belches softly and then the guy from LA screams:

'Fucken asshole Ostralians,' from the bottom of the stairs and they all giggle and Marilyn grabs Twentiethcentury and Liz by the hand and drags them away in a springy triangular formation and Marilyn's eyes leapfrog around in the strange blue light and stringy strands of words like:

'Where's Malcolm?'

And:

'There's Humphrey the wonderfully eloquent statement-maker Bogart,' zoom and zap from Marilyn's motormouth in all the neck-snapping light-headed confusion and thoughts like:

Twentiethcentury seemed taller at the restaurant,

And:

He seemed younger on television,

Needle and noodle behind her I-can't-stop-smiling frozen face and her eyes get stuck to Liz's shiny gold loopy earrings and then she reaches out for Twentiethcentury's hand and squeezes his limp pudgy fingers and rubs his sweaty palms and her teeth grind and her tongue whirligigs and she nearly chokes on another glob of sour yuck and swallows dryly and her neck snaps stiffly as she leans over and nibbles on a

170

furry lobe but that's when—

Oops—

She lets go of Humphrey's hand and spits out his ear and swivels around looking for Twentiethcentury who seems to have disappeared and Humphrey shouts:

'He's over at the bar,' eloquently and wonderfully and wraps an arm around her shoulders and hugs and squeezes and rubs and pats and smiles his very nice slightly-bucked-teeth-with-calcium-spots smile and points out all the celebrities but Marilyn's not really sure who they are and just smiles an enormous I-can't-stop-smiling smile and that's when Twentiethcentury comes back and hands her a glass of water and then asks her to hold his glass while he pops two white pills—

Slurp—

And then grunts:

'This place is incredible like man I mean two bucks for a glass of water?' in that no-I-never-did-have-my-adenoids-out-so-yes-I-do-have-a-sinus-condition accent in her ear and Marilyn can't help smiling at all the snortling gruff—

Huhs—

And the heavy breathing and the way he keeps twisting his head to one side and cracking his neck while he talks and all she wants to do is wrap him up in her arms and press her face close to his and drink cups of hot chocolate in a big bouncy brass bed and then Marilyn's eyes get stuck to Twentiethcentury's and Twentiethcentury says:

'I'm kind of getting a little burned out by all this loud music you know?'

And pulls at his tie while his eyes tick and blink

from his shiny wet face and he licks his lips which are too big and too red and too soft and—

Slurps—

On his water and Marilyn nods all restless twitching and ready-to-go enthusiasm and Twentiethcentury takes her hand and smiles and belches softly and tugs Marilyn towards the door and Marilyn grabs onto Liz who grabs onto Humphrey and finally they're all squinting and wincing and writhing slide-specimens in the overbearingly bright icy grey early morning light.

Humphrey pulls out a pair of Blues Brothers glasses and Liz drops her head in her hands and cries out and Twentiethcentury's bent over double and moaning:

'Oh man this mono shit sucks.'

And Marilyn holds onto a pole and gasps in helpless agony while two red hot iron pokers bore through her eyes and bury deep into the back of her head where they smoulder just two tiny white dots and somebody asks that unfortunate what-time-is-it? question and Liz looks up from her hands and still smiling this I-can't-stop-smiling smile says:

'7.30 a.m.'

And that's when Twentiethcentury starts sobbing almost crying:

'Oh no oh no.'

And Marilyn's standing there with her eyes closed watching two tiny dots go pink and yellow and green and white like fireworks and meanwhile Twentiethcentury's hunched over double and snorting and huffing and puffing and grunts out:

'Oh no I don't believe this are you sure is that really the time oh shit I gotta go I gotta get a cab oh man I've got two hours oh shit I've got a plane to catch fucken 7.30.'

172

And then Twentiethcentury moans and doubles over and farts loudly and mushily and says:

'Oh man,' and runs back to the club and Liz and Humphrey start laughing and lean their heads together as tears run down their cheeks and their knees all jelly make them wobble and tremble and the two hot pokers have Marilyn pinned to the spot and she doesn't know what to think of Twentiethcentury and his wind problem and meanwhile she can hear Inspector Jacques Clouseau say:

The Monsieur is feeling a little bit flatulent today.

And wants to laugh but can't and it's all the hot pokers' fault and at the same time she still can't stop smiling and her cheeks—

Ouch—

Are beginning to ache but somehow it all seems worthwhile now that she has Twentiethcentury and now that she knows he's been looking for her and that he didn't just send her the dozen long-stemmed reds and the note out of embarassment and pity and Marilyn senses something strange going on around her loins at the idea of going back to Twentiethcentury's place for a little snooze and brekkie even if he does seem a little weird and it's a shame he's not feeling well but—

Silly me he's got a plane to catch—

And Marilyn opens her eyes which feels a little bit like peeling off two toenails—

Aaargh—

And so she closes them again and clings swaying slightly to the pole in the chilly wind on the snowy street.

Meanwhile Twentiethcentury's back on the can rubbing his steaming forehead with his hand and blinking away sweat and tears all twitchingly tickled by the prickling perspiration running down his neck and then he groans and loses everything in a rush:

'Oh man,' and then sighs all empty and dizzy and passes out into thick wads of cotton wool.

And that's when the guy in the tux grabs Twentiethcentury's shoulders and someone else grabs his legs and they drag him out onto the footpath where they drop him sneeringly:

'Fucken asshole Ostralians,' into the hard snowy cold.

And it's not long before—

Oh oh—

Humphrey notices the noisy cooing crowd and untangles himself from Liz and rushes over to Twentiethcentury who's just coming round all dazed and mumbling:

'Marilyn,' over and over and Humphrey helps him up and:

'Shoo shoo,' shoos all the noisy cooers eloquently away and then:

'Yo!' hails a cab and shuffles Marilyn wonderfully in the back seat and slides Twentiethcentury eloquently in next and slams the door shut and then Humphrey and Liz stand waving and blowing kisses as the cab speeds off into the overbearingly bright glare all screeching and sliding down the icy white wrong side of the road.

And Twentiethcentury lies down and nestles his head in Marilyn's lap and Marilyn watches the grey buildings fly past through the two intensely hot pokers and—

Poor baby—

Gazes down all tender concern at Twentiethcentury's jaded world-weary face which is all red and puffy around the tightly closed clam eyes and unshaven furrowed and frowning and transformed plasticine up close and she's just about to kiss him for the first time when—

Eeech—

He yawns and she nearly gags on the garlic and ginger and fermenting dead animal stench and peeks inside at his perfect white baby teeth and that's when Twentiethcentury's upside down sideways mouth says:

'Why don't you come to Washington with me?'

And Marilyn smiles in the stench and her teeth hurt full of holes and her cheeks ache and she really wants to go to Washington with Twentiethcentury and doesn't want to go home any more so she says:

'That'd be great.'

And Twentiethcentury falls asleep into a warm snuffling place of furrowed frown lines and swelling pulsating pudgy cheeks and grinding teeth.

The city speeds by all bouncing grey and lilac and a chilly breeze blows around piles of stuffed black plastic garbage bags and yesterday's snow.

Meanwhile the beast keeps on grumbling and rumbling down wet drains on subway trains and oozes hot steam.

And watches through its thousand invisible eyes.

And sends Marilyn a little warning that she doesn't heed.

And Marilyn thinks:

Peach margaritas and nightclubs and parties and hot chilli dip and museums and movie stars and Wall Street and the Chrysler Building and the icy white wrong side of the road.

And a very different sort of smile begins to play around the corners of her lippy mouth at the first insidious symbiotic pull of this sweet dreamy mythical place and Marilyn sighs all seduced and caught in a spell.

And then the driver says:

'Corner of West Broadway and Canal,' and Twentiethcentury sits up groggy and starts rummaging through his pockets and then he snorts:

'Oh man,' and huffs and says:

'Have you got five bucks? I don't know I can't seem to find my wallet.'

And Marilyn begins to rummage around in her pockets and pulls out two subway tokens and an Australian twenty-dollar note and giggles:

'A lobster.'

And Twentiethcentury's still wondering about the lobster:

'You mean a crayfish?' when the driver switches off the engine and shakes his head and—

Thump thump—

Thumps on the steering wheel and finally Twentiethcentury says:

'Do you take cards?'

And the driver shrugs:

'Of course we take cards you schmuck.'

Marilyn smiles and climbs out and slides ankle-deep in slushy snow and her eyes are two red running holes now that the pokers have gone away and she sneezes and buries her hands deep in her pockets and breathes all steamy and smiles and licks her dry chapped lips and Twentiethcentury takes her hand and grunts and snorts:

176

'We'll go upstairs take a shower grab a gyro platter and get a car to pick us up and drive us to Newark OK?'

And Marilyn nods and follows Twentiethcentury into the rattling old goods lift and through the labyrinth of hallways and offices to an arched doorway and gasps:

'Wow,' at Twentiethcentury's home sweet converted-basketball-court home and Twentiethcentury snorts:

'It's a little raw but I kind of like it that way you know?' and rushes from the humidifier to the TV to the video to the answering machine switching things on and trailing a dirty wet snow puddle all over the polished parquet floor.

And meanwhile Marilyn squelches—

Squelch squelch—

Over to the TV and is just about to turn it off in anticipation of hours of watering eyes and sniffling nose but that's when—

Zing—

A song by REM is playing on MTV and she's not sure why but the song sends shivers down her spine and all of a sudden she just wants to stand up and yell although she doesn't—

Wow—

And by force of habit she's just about to start rubbing her nasal cavities red raw and scratching holes in her eyes and expects to lose contact completely with the involuntary muscles which regulate her lungs at any second when something goes—

Click—

And the world as we know it dissolves into black with a high—

177

Marilyn's Almost Terminal New York Adventure

Beep.

And it's the end of the world as we know it and the end of Marilyn's allergy to TV all in one momentous earth-shattering blow.

Marilyn looks out the window and watches a beaten-up yellow cab pull up at a red light on the dirty snow and thinks how great it is not to be allergic to TV any more although she wonders whether it was the cab ride into Manhattan from JFK and the deadly pothole and the subsequent short-lived bout of concussion that's responsible or if it's meeting Twentiethcentury and she can't decide which is more likely but then her thoughts take off in a different direction and she wonders whether it's all TV that she's cured of or if it's just American TV or just video clips or just that particular shiver-sending song so she watches a few more clips and her nose and eyes are still dry but she won't be able to find out if she's allergic to Australian TV until she gets back home if she ever even wants to go back now that she's found Twentiethcentury so that probably means she's cured for good or at least for as long as she stays in America and that starts her wondering if there's something different about the TV here and if there's different kinds of TV or is there just something in the air in NYC that's different and then she remembers how the image on TV back home is so infested with white noise and so many generations old that the picture is close to disappearing completely but she still can't work it out and it still doesn't seem to add up and in the end she's simply and absolutely glad that she can watch TV now and it feels good to be a member of the world's biggest social club even if it means a terribly significant part of her is dead and gone forever and ever.

And when the cab pulls away Marilyn finds herself staring straight into the thousand invisible smiling eyes of Manhattan the twin-brontosaurus-headed beast.

And that's when she discovers herbality and the beast looks unconvinced but Marilyn doesn't care and—

Oh—

Is born again or born anew or reborn or becomes somebody else or is resurrected from the dead because even the end of the world as we know it and the end of a debilitating but fashionable allergy to TV isn't the end of everything.

And meanwhile a nasal answering-machine voice says:

'Hi Twentiethcentury sweetheart it's me Garbo and I'm at my parents' house on Long Island escaping from everything for a couple of days and like you know after everything that's happened I just thought I might.'

And Marilyn instantly recognises Garbo's God-are-they-silicon? tits voice and crumbles all raspberry shortbread at the thought of nasty forks that stab the hands of innocent waifs and meanwhile Garbo says:

'And like I've been so upset I've been shopping you know purchasing like with my credit record? Anyway I had to buy so I bought this new answering machine that stores the time people call automatically and gets their number and you can program it to phone your messages through when you're at work or out of town and so you can see why I had to have one and I've been waiting and waiting for you to call but you haven't and no-one's called me yet and I'm beginning to wonder whether it works or not so could you call me some time you know if you have time?'

179

And then there's a—
Beep—
And a few seconds of static and Twentiethcentury's huffing puffing heavy breathing while everything freezes.

And then Marilyn or Marilyn's image or Marilyn's ghost says:

'That's a great song you know by REM do you know what it's called?'

And Twentiethcentury says:

'What it's called? I don't know.'

And pads off to the bathroom trailing the phone on a long extension lead.

Later on at the cafe Twentiethcentury ticks and blinks over the mountainous munchable terrain of his gyro platter and grunts:

'You know huh there was something about you I felt from the first moment I saw you like I don't know some kind of attraction and OK I know it sounds trite and maybe even cliché but believe me Marilyn huh it's true you know?'

And then Twentiethcentury takes a mouth-splitting bite and drops a red tomato sauce baby—
Plop—
In a manger of reconstituted French fries.

And meanwhile Twentiethcentury's words send a cold desperate bolt of desolate windswept inevitability shooting through Marilyn's busty blonde frame and she reaches across the red and white checked table-cloth and takes hold of Twentiethcentury's stumpy pink hairy hand all greasy with mayonnaise and reconstituted French fries:

'Oh Twentiethcentury you're so romantic,' and gulps down her additional cawfee and sighs.

As Marilyn stares across the table into his round brown eyes all moist and mesmerising between their sea-anemone lashes she feels something strange happen down around her loins at the idea of a night in a hotel with Twentiethcentury in Washington—

Mmm—

And her heart fills with yearning lusting longing and the Christmas beetles and crispy cicada shells shout:

Olé!

And start clicking their maracas and stomping a passionate bolero down her digestive tract as if she's still the same Marilyn she was when she first arrived but the sweet nostalgic wave of lust doesn't last long and it passes as nostalgia always tends to do.

Meanwhile Twentiethcentury takes his molars through their early morning aerobics class:

> *One two one two*
> *Staying alive*
> *Staying alive.*

And he's almost finished his mouthful when he says:

'You know like I think Wall Street types tend to be loners I mean with my history of broken hearts huh.'

And chomps and chews and pushes bits of food back in with both hands and:

'Excuse me,' belches softly.

Marilyn finds her eyes drifting down to the mountainous munchable terrain of his gyro platter—

Oh my God—

And the newly herbal Marilyn's not sure whether she's seeing things or whether Twentiethcentury really is eating his way through rolling green fields of crisp lettuce and whole mounds of tomatoes and tussocky hillocks of coleslaw and potato salad and a pool of fried egg and rivers of tomato sauce and mayonnaise dotted with nuggets of fatty sliced sausage and lashings of reconstituted potato French fries and Marilyn starts thinking about heart disease and varicose veins and colon cancer and cellulite and high blood pressure and she's just about to tell him all about herbality and the predictable proliferation of all things cooked in salt sugar and fat when Twentiethcentury says:

'I guess like a true Wall Street type I look for value in my relationships I mean I'm always on the lookout for a new deal you know especially for my poetry like a muse or inspiration or something but I also see true value in a person who can cook the sorts of things that keep the old juices flowing you know? like maybe a little homemade coleslaw with reduced-cholesterol oil or some steamed vegetables with sesame seeds or some tofu or something like that.'

And then Twentiethcentury smiles greasily and reaches under the table and squeezes Marilyn's knee and fixes her with one of his jaded world-weary looks and licks some sauce from the corners of his mouth and snorts and grunts:

'Because like if you don't eat you don't shit and if you don't shit you die do you understand what I'm saying here?'

But Marilyn can't hear anything over the electrifying thrilling trilling of her heart and this time the nostalgia grips her fiercely by the throat and who cares about colon cancer anyway? as her own personalised juices start pumping pulsing and pounding to some biodynamic Bacchic get-up-and-boogie beat of their own and it's just as if she never died at all and everything's just as before even though it's different as well.

It's only once Manhattan the beast spits them out into the shuttle flight-filled sky all hurt and abandoned to see Marilyn leaving so soon and then after Twentieth-century kisses Marilyn all fatty sausages and onion rings for the first time and whispers a minimalist poem in her ear:

> *I want you*
> *You're mine*
> *Take me.*

And disappears belching with indigestion that Marilyn begins to think seriously about herbality and the end of the world and to wonder if there's anything anyone can do and places her nostalgia firmly on the back burner for a while.

later on in Washington when Twentiethcentury goes to his meeting Marilyn wanders across the chilly desolate windswept Mall towards the burnt orange horizon beneath the yawning post-nuclear-holocaust end-of-the-world sky.

As the wind whips her hair around her mouth and her face glows golden in the aftermath of the blast Marilyn or her image or her ghost finds herself ranting and raving all King Lear in a teacup as everything she's ever heard or read about Vegans and Greenies comes whispering back:

'Well the thing is that we all eat too much meat and the environment just can't supply us with a giant-sized slab of prime beef steak every day and if you think about it you don't really need to eat meat every day because what about like the Italian peasants you know who lived on pasta and bread and vegetables and only ate tiny amounts of meat and yet now people really freak out if they don't eat meat every day and someone once told me this girl who's really into naturopathy that you get the best concentration of protein when you eat soya beans and biodynamic brown rice and suddenly it just seems so obvious that meat is just this really really decadent unnecessary thing and only the sort of thing you need to eat once a week and so.'

And meanwhile miles away Manhattan the beast with a thousand invisible eyes and twin bronze bronto-

ranting and
raving all King
Lear in a teacup

saurus heads crouches patiently awaiting Marilyn's return at the edge of the water guarding the grey expanse where the two mighty rivers meet and belches and rumbles its rusty pipes and oozes sulphurous steam through countless gurgling drains.

And Marilyn stares out into the burnt orange horizon:

'And like that's the other side to this dreamy mythical place because like if we keep chopping down all the trees without putting anything back then you know pretty soon it's going to be the end of the world as we know it and wow I don't think I'll ever be able to work nine-to-five or eat red meat again.'

And that's when Marilyn catches sight of R. what-the-fuck-does-the-R.-stand-for? Hudson another lonely figure all golden and glowing in the aftermath of the blast.

And then R. what-the-fuck-does-the-R.-stand-for? Hudson asks her what she's seen in Washington so far and Marilyn sexily squints up her eyes and stares off into a hazy middle distance and murmurs something vague and unintelligible so R. says:

'Detail,' and then he pauses for effect although Marilyn isn't sure exactly what kind of effect he's pausing for until he goes on to say:

'I mean detail's umm very important like I sometimes think about what it's done for me like you'd never believe I was selling crack on Wall Street only four years ago.'

And then he asks her to guess the name of America's most important detail and when Marilyn sexily squints up her eyes and stares off into a hazy middle distance again he says impatiently:

'The Smithsonian.'

And then tells her that she should study the contents of the Mall with a writerly eye for detail and that in particular she should concentrate on the National Air and Space Museum because of all the great details they have in there and then he waves goodbye and says:

'I'll see you back in New York oh and don't forget to go and see the Jackie Gleeson retrospective when you're there OK?'

And as Marilyn watches him disappear into all the burnt orange slushy snow she works out how much sleep she's had since New Year's Eve and Durrell's party which doesn't add up to a whole hell of a lot of shut-eye and then she stumbles past the security guards into the National Air and Space Museum and stops in front of a missile display.

But then—

Oh my God—

That's when Marilyn's peripheral vision catches a glimpse of a tall thin woman in a very creased baggy linen suit on the other side of the display:

Virginia.

And a cold shiver runs down her spine as the woman who might be Virginia disappears behind a large sign that says:

V–2 LONG RANGE BALLISTIC MISSILE

Originally designated A–K, the German V–2 was a milestone in the progress of rocket technology which had begun with Robert H. Goddard's flight in 1926. The V–2 represented an advanced level of rocket engine technology which did not exist in other countries. Based on this German accomplishment, thermonuclear warheads have since revolutionised strategic warfare.

The V–2 held the promise of space flight. The line of engine development from the V–2 through the Ridstone missile to the Saturn series of space launch vehicle is clear and direct. The V–2 was developed by a team of engineers working under Wernher von Braun at Pecunwunde on the Baltic Sea. Four thousand of these rockets were fired against Allied targets in England and on the continent in 1944–5. After World War II, captured V–2 rockets were used to train technicians in large missile launch procedure, and were the first US large sounding rockets to carry scientific instrument payloads into the upper atmosphere.

And when Marilyn finally looks up there's no trace of the tall thin woman in the very creased baggy linen suit who might be Virginia and Marilyn's not sure whether she's more shocked about the V–2 Long Range Ballistic Missile display or about Virginia's unique talent for the Clayton's appearance which is much more of a disappearance or semi-apparent appearance than a straightforward appearance.

And as Marilyn brushes away creeping cobwebs of murky menace she bumps into a life-size replica of the Challenger Space Shuttle and then stumbles out onto the slushy snowy streets of the Mall.

Back out under the windswept post-nuclear-holocaust sky Marilyn rants and raves all King Lear in a
teacup again:

'You know like what about the Challenger Space
Shuttle disaster and the human fallibility factor and
like Washington is just a giant Egyptian-style tomb full of
one-size-fits-all one-of-a-kinds from all over the world and
now the crew of the space shuttle are heroes and the
program just keeps on going and somehow it's the end of
the world unless we stop eating meat every day.'

And all these thoughts are just whirring around all
free-form stream of consciousness until she climbs into the
back of a cab and the driver smiles hello in the mirror and
then says:

'So who do you think'll win the next election?'

And when Marilyn doesn't answer he answers for
her and then runs through a list of candidates and
Marilyn's not really sure if she can believe him or not
because most of the candidates sound like movie stars and
film directors and really the identity of the future President is the last thing on her mind because all she can
think about as she slides around on the gargantuan
vinyl seat is Virginia and:

What is *Virginia doing in Washington?*

Anyway.

b ack in their hotel room Marilyn lets Twentiethcentury undress her and then she undresses him
and that's when she finally comes face to face
with his beneath-the-appearance dishevelled self and
cradles the jaded world-weary look about his face after
travelling halfway around the world to meet him after
seeing him make one of his historic television appearances
on a matinee show and more.

And while Marilyn caresses the tight curly knots of
dark fur on Twentiethcentury's stomach with the tip of
her tongue and sniffs—

Mmm—

And sighs and moans Twentiethcentury massages
her neck and—

Ouch—

Pinches the tiny tight nerves around her shoulders and
slowly but surely she feels all the confusion and
anxiety of the last few days flowing out of her body and
probably making a puddle on the crisp white linen sheet.

And Marilyn moans:

'Oh Twentieth-century.'

And Twentieth-century grunts back:

'Huh?'

And Marilyn says:

'Have you mmm ever thought aaahh about cutting down on the umm mmm

what transformed

plasticine face

Twentieth-

century's like

in bed

191

on the ummm the ummm mmm meat you eat?'

And Twentiethcentury says:

'Uh uh.'

And that's when Marilyn finds out—

Ohhh—

What transformed plasticine face Twentiethcentury's like in bed and ummms and ahhhhs all the way through their sensually intense:

'Oh Twentiethcentury you're so safe,' safe sexual encounter.

And later on Marilyn's sitting on top of Twentiethcentury who's lying face-down all sweaty and massagebegging so Marilyn gives Twentiethcentury the first massage she's ever given in her life and can't help feeling a little embarrassed about massaging someone she's only just met but—

What the hell?

So she pummels and drools over his blackheadspotted shoulders and plays dot-to-dot with her tongue on the freckles on his white hairless back and nibbles and sucks up and down each side of his short stocky neck and tongue kisses each vertebra all the way down his fleshy spine to the dark furry pool that trickles into the smooth brown crevice between each pink pimply cheek of his plump rump and:

'Oh Marilyn.'

And Twentiethcentury suddenly rolls over and waves his stiff little finger all dishevelled and naked and:

'Oh Twentiethcentury.'

And the evening passes as such evenings always do.

Later that night over dinner which is the last meal the newly herbal Marilyn ever eats that has meat in it and yes the frogs' legs in lemon grass and coconut sauce are delicious and after a bottle of champagne and a few cognacs Marilyn toasts:

'To the last meat I'll ever eat.'

And Twentiethcentury says:

'To the last drink you'll ever meet.'

And then they stumble back up to their hotel room all drunk and exhausted where they have another sensually intense safe sexual encounter and this time they try a 66 99 which Marilyn enjoys a lot more than their previous flat on your back missionary position although she's a little turned off when Twentiethcentury starts dribbling beer all over her and licking it off and:

'Oh Twentiethcentury,' isn't incredibly impressed when the banana goes soft and mushy and breaks into lots of little pieces that Twentiethcentury can't seem to suck out:

'How's that?'

'Nice.'

'Oops.'

'What?'

'The bananas keep breaking and getting stuck in there.'

Yuck.

And Marilyn giggles and can't seem to get into the idea of sucking honey from Twentiethcentury's pink dark haired nipples but somehow it's all a lot of fun and a lot of personal barriers get broken down and turned inside out and torn apart and shoved at the back of linen closets and then Twentiethcentury farts and moans:

'Oh man,' and runs off to the bathroom.

And Marilyn lies there vaguely chapped with mushy

bananas oozing from between her legs and indulges in a little herbal fantasy where she and Twentiethcentury are united in their mutual understanding of environmental issues and only eat meat once a week and have renounced all forms of artificial stimulants and survive on whole foods and herbal teas and spend whole days at a stretch snuggled up in a king-size futon bed with 100% cotton sheets and a goose down quilt and feather pillows sipping cups of tepid soya milk and honey watching the snow fall and reading poetry in a simple bare room without a TV or a humidifier or an answering machine or a video machine or a central heating facility or a refrigerator that runs on those gases that are fucking up the ozone and only a little natural gas burner to heat cans of beans and soya milk and water for herbal tea.

And then Twentiethcentury comes back and says:

'Have you flossed yet?'

And Marilyn hasn't so she follows Twentiethcentury into the bathroom and wonders what evil chemicals and artificial fibres the body is forced to deal with in the form of dental floss and says:

'Have you ever thought of getting some herbal dental floss?'

But Twentiethcentury hasn't and doesn't seem to see Marilyn's point as he teaches his little blue-eyed big-busted Ossie girl how to floss.

And then back in bed Marilyn sort of forgets about herbality and gets lost in Twentiethcentury and his TV-matinee jaded world-weary look and just before they fall asleep Marilyn says:

'Did I ever tell you about the movie star?' thinking of faces and TV screens and Twentiethcentury says:

'No.'

And then Marilyn tells him all about the movie star:

'Last night I met a movie star and he wanted to show me his gyroscope.'

'Who was it?'

'I don't know.'

'You don't know?'

'I knew his face but I couldn't remember his name.'

'What did he look like?'

'Dark hair pale skin stubble intense.'

'Oh.'

'I wish I could remember his name.'

And Marilyn doesn't pay much attention when Twentiethcentury suddenly bursts into a hot sweat all teeth-grinding anxiety and blinking ticking eyes and she's just about to drift off to sleep in herbal la la land when Twentiethcentury gruffly grunts in that no-I-never-did-have-my-adenoids-out-so-yes-I-do-have-a-sinus-condition accent:

'You know I'd really appreciate it if you'd make a list of names and places and dates of all the people you've ever slept with including surnames because you know like you just can't be too careful these days.'

And Marilyn goes all cold and goose bumpy and begins to taste a dry blood taste in the back of her throat and thinks:

What does he mean names and places and dates of everyone I've ever slept with?

And even though Marilyn wants to say a lot of hurt insulted and defensive things she clamps up like an angry red ball deeply in that's-the-last-straw shock and watches stupefied while her herbal dreams shatter into a trillion million pieces amazed that:

I can't believe he said what I think he just said.

Twentiethcentury could turn out to be so deeply entrenched in decadence and fascism and the patriarchy and completely the wrong sort of guy for her:

Oh shit.

And while Twentiethcentury chomps and grinds his teeth and takes his sinuses through the paces of their nightly sniffling wheezing gymnastics Marilyn lies awake accusingly—

You meat-eating decadent sexist Wall Street pig—

Tossing and turning and:

You deserve all the indigestion you get—

Cursing and cussing.

When she does finally fall asleep into la la land it's not a herbal paradise at all but instead Marilyn finds herself lost in a nightmarish place of tombs full of biting mosquitoes and mummies' curses and Virginia has something to do with it all although when Marilyn wakes up:

'Room service good morning,' she's not sure what or whether Twentiethcentury really said what she thinks he said last night so while she contemplates her three-course herbal breakfast of:

sundried fruit, and:

unsweetened natural muesli, and:

100% natural soya milk, and:

goat's milk yogurt, and:

lemon zinger tea—

Everything's a little bit unsure and so-what's-new? confusing.

And things get even more confusing when Marilyn sits back and watches Twentiethcentury launch into mountains of fried onion rings and second helpings of fried eggs and hash browns and tiny spicy pork link sausages and coffee and a pumpernickel bagel with cream cheese onion rings capers and smoked salmon:

Wow.

And Marilyn picks at her herbal breakfast and makes lame attempts at conversation with Twentieth-century no-longer-the-man-of-her-dreams Fox like:

'I love swimming.'

And:

'You know I think swimming is an aphrodisiac.'

And:

'Do you think I should give up alcohol as well?'

And Twentiethcentury just keeps on reinforcing all her disappointed conclusions by saying things like:

'Oh yeah?'

And:

'Huh.'

And:

'Have you ever tried hash browns with onion rings?'

And:

'Have some of this pumpernickel bagel with lox it's delicious.'

And Marilyn looks at him and narrows her eyes and then she says:

'So you're not going to give up meat?'

And Twentiethcentury snorts:

'What is it with you with all this meat stuff all of a sudden?'

And Marilyn says:

'Well it's just that I don't think the environment can support us all if we eat meat every day and anyway the best source of protein is soya beans and rice because

the amino acids in meat sort of cancel each other out and
this friend of mine who's a naturopath said—'

And Twentiethcentury says:

'I didn't know you were you know like a neo-hippie I
mean yesterday you were drinking coffee and like last
night you were eating meat so what's the fucken story all
of a sudden?'

And Marilyn says:

'Well I'm giving up as from today.'

And Twentiethcentury leans back and says:

'Well you see like huh when I started on Wall Street
something happened to me you know I mean like my
digestive system just kind of packed up and left and
like my doctor got me onto hi-fibre low-cholesterol
foods but huh like I'm no neo-hippie health freak I just
get a little tired of the predictable proliferation of all
things cooked in salt sugar and fat but that doesn't
mean I want to eat steamed vegetables and tofu every
night do you understand what I'm saying here I love
food you know?'

And Marilyn says:

'Oh,' all wet sulky eyes.

Twentiethcentury leans forward and spears another
tiny spicy pork link sausage and says:

'Look honey try one of these sausages they're delicious
honest.'

And—

Sluuurp—

Slurps his coffee and Marilyn shakes her head and
sighs bitterly disappointed that his beneath-the-appearance dishevelled self and the jaded world-weary look
about his face are just appearances once more which
conceal his deeper decadent fascist and patriarchal self

which is not very romantic or attractive at all and even though it might just be another appearance and not a true self Marilyn is so turned off she can barely finish her breakfast.

Twentiethcentury's almost finished his mouthful of tiny spicy pork link sausages and fried onion rings when he snorts and grunts:

'So have you thought any more about what I said last night?'

Marilyn stalls for time:

'What do you mean?'

And sexily squints up her eyes and stares off into a hazy middle distance reluctant to hear her life so far reduced to what sounds like a reading list for an adult education course in modern literature and female sexuality:

Miller

Durrell

Lawrence

And shrugs her shoulders.

And then Twentiethcentury says:

'Because I don't know how much further I can go with this till I have all the facts and figures I mean like for the moment I'm afraid the deal's off and like believe me I don't like this any more than you but what's the point of paying all those expensive fees to a personal attorney if you never take their advice?'

And swallows his mouthful and wipes his fingers on her bare knee:

'My sweet little Ossie girl.'

Then groans and hurries to the bathroom clutching his silk paisley bathrobe and a pile of figures to ponder in solitude.

And Marilyn says:

'Serves you right,' all smug and stuffed with sun-dried fruit and sipping lemon zinger tea—

Yuck—

And—

Fuck that for a bad joke.

And later out in the glittering gilt and marble floored lots-of-luscious-green-potted-plants filled hotel lobby Twentiethcentury wraps her in his arms and holds her tight and Marilyn melts helplessly and whispers:

'Tell me something about yourself Twentieth-century.'

'You mean like my poetry?'

'Tell me things.'

'What kind of things?'

'You know like things anything.'

'You know how I feel about you.'

'That's not what I mean.'

'Then what do you mean?'

'Tell me something about you I don't already know something you've never told anyone else.'

'I can't think of anything.'

'Please.'

'Well look I can't open up to a person until I know them and trust them and that may take a little time and like why is it that women are always on at me to open up?'

And Twentiethcentury leans back and Marilyn catches a flash of something small and dark and hurt like a little boy in his eyes and that's when—

Oh oh—

Something starts twisting her insides around while something else in there is expanding fit to explode and Marilyn suddenly doubles over in pain and the taxi arrives and someone in a silly soldier suit picks up their bags and someone else holds the door open and then —

Oh no —

As soon as she sits down in the back of the cab she involuntarily emits a foul odious jet of warm farting air and —

Oh my God —

Has to wind down the window and then —

Ooops —

She emits another warm farting jet and that's when she starts giggling out of control and Marilyn doesn't notice when the driver raises his eyes at Twentiethcentury and gestures with his head and says:

'She Ostralian?' because she can't stop her giggling or her warm emissions and she doesn't notice when Twentiethcentury winds down his window and looks at her surprised and suspicious or when the driver winds down his window with a knowing wink and Marilyn giggles all the way to the airport which is more than half an hour of Washington expressway and the first thing she does hear is the driver saying:

'People are sheer stark raving crazy nuts quote me,' and wipes the tears from her eyes.

Marilyn spends most of the flight back to New York in a tiny tinny toilet cubicle with Twentiethcentury's poem:

> *Darling Marilyn,*
>
> *You didn't need to spell it out*
> *I knew what was occurring*

Marilyn's Almost Terminal New York Adventure

I ask myself: who is in charge?
Your Goethe—my Goering?

Moments connect, time slows and stops
I hope there is no victor:
Oh black hole open up: abyss!
(There is no scale Herr Richter.)

Your gentle touch: my hair's a mess
Oh no! Not this again!
And wait the day immortal words:
Please can't we still be friends?

Flee daunting thought not to return
I say: there'll be no battle:
To have the spoils and miss the rest
That would not test our mettle.

These kisses last and linger on
As searching eyes all gleam and shine,
In love-stuck gaze all chat and talk
Yet, silence best we do divine.

When meaning comes and leaves all time
Each pindrop gaze it seems anew
Less strangers now—and less is more
And more, like me and you.

Twentiethcentury S. Fox Jnr

And the plane goes—
  Buck buck toss toss—
  Through all the chilly airpockets.

When she sits back down in her window seat Twentiethcentury says:

'Do you know any love poems?'

And Marilyn recites the first thing that comes into her mind:

> *The day you came into my life*
> *The way you came into my life.*

Which are the first two lines of Durrell's favourite John Laws poem that is absolutely indispensable in these sorts of situations and then Twentiethcentury says:

'That's kind of neat do you know any more?'

But Marilyn doesn't and shakes her head and looks out the window.

And that's when—

Oh my God—

Marilyn comes face to face with Manhattan the beast with its thousand invisible eyes and twin bronze brontosaurus heads yet again as it peers shortsighted into the steamy fog and crouches patiently at the edge of the water guarding the grey expanse where the two mighty rivers meet with the grey towers of Midtown lurking hungry in the background like older relatives and gloats:

I told you so.

And Twentiethcentury doesn't see the beast and leans over and points with a stumpy dark-haired pink finger at one of the ugly many-eyed heads and says:

'That's where I work.'

And that's when—

Ping—

A little yellow light switches on in Marilyn's head

203

and she settles back in her seat and suddenly it's the end of Twentiethcentury Fox and the end of the world and the end of her allergy and the end of TV and the end of herbality.

Back in Liz's apartment everything's a crazy bustling confusion of Liz and her sisters and her flatmates and all of their I'm-so-pissed-off-about-being-evicted boxes and suitcases and Marilyn's strangely reassured when she finds Liz in the middle of it all hand-blow-drying real potato French fries and then when Liz asks about Twentiethcentury with a knowing look beneath her dyed natural hair Marilyn shrugs and says:

'Oh well.'

And they both sigh and sip on their Coronas and gulp down shots of tequila.

And then Liz says:

'Let's get this show on the road kid.'

And leads a post-herbal more alive Marilyn to the bathroom with the no-longer-phenomenal sink with no plug and hands her a cleaning rag and a jar of generic non-brand powder cleanser and it isn't long before Marilyn stops pretending to clean the sink and meets her eyes in the smeary cracked mirror and touches her pinkly flushed furry peach cheek and looks from one eye to the other and thinks how small and alone she is and she runs a white-as-porcelain finger back and forth over the softest skin she's ever felt and a cold shiver runs down her spine and goose bumps make her hair prickle and the beginnings of a tear form in the corner of each eye.

Damn.

Somewhere between the second and third round of peach and lime now-we're-on-the-streets-kids margaritas in the second or third where-the-fuck-are-we-going-to-sleep-tomorrow-night? bar Marilyn smiles a brave weary smile at Liz and her flatmates and heads off to the bathroom.

And Marilyn closes the frosted glass panelled door and stands in front of the mirror amidst all the noisy graffiti under the sordid blue neon lights and—

Oh well—

Thinks about Twentiethcentury.

And it's a little bit like coming out of deep sleep and holding onto the last part of a dream because Twentiethcentury's face has become a little featureless and Marilyn can only vaguely remember his beneath-the-appearance dishevelled self and the jaded world-weary look about his face and then—

Oh Twentieth-century—

Marilyn smells the sweet oily smell on Twentieth-century's cheeks and sees his transformed plasticine face all warm shiny fluttering eyelashes and then sighs:

a croaky voice

crackles electrically

from the occupied

cubicle in the

sordid late late

atmosphere

205

'*Au revoir*,' and shakes her head.

And the first cubicle hasn't got any paper so Marilyn goes into the second cubicle and while she's lining the seat with paper she hears someone else come in and slam the frosted glass panelled door and then she hears the tinkle of keys and then another shuddering slam as someone slams the door to the cubicle with no paper.

And then:

'Ohhhhhhhh,' and a deep sigh like groan oozes from the next cubicle and Marilyn decides against a long sit thinking about Twentiethcentury and the end of the world and going home and hurries back out to the mirror and while she's quickly dabbing on some lipstick she hears another deep sigh like groan and then a croaky voice crackles electrically from the occupied cubicle in the sordid late late atmosphere:

'Oh God I'll never find her.'

And Marilyn decides to ignore this remark as all the stories she's ever heard about crazies in New York and muggings and weirdos all come rushing back in a series of delirious hallucinations of knives and blood and needles and she's just about to leave when the voice croaks on and crackles electrically:

'You see I'll never find her in a crazy place like this and everything will be a complete and utter and ultimate waste of time and money and energy and it'll mean everything's pointless and that life has no meaning because everything you do always fucks up anyway and I only came here to find this friend of mine despite the once-in-a-lifetime employment opportunity that I couldn't say no to and if I don't find her I'm going to look like some kind of has-been no-hoper village idiot when I go home so now I can't even go home can I?'

And Marilyn goes to say something but senses another meaning behind the words although she's not exactly sure what sort of meaning behind which particular words and so she stops herself from saying anything and shakes her head instead.

But the voice presses on and pins her down and pushes her up against a wall:

'Are you still there hello?'

So Marilyn says the only thing she can say which is:

'Sorry were you talking to me?'

And the voice says:

'Yes I was talking to you.'

And Marilyn says:

'Oh I thought you must have been talking to someone else.'

And then there's a long pregnant menacing pause and Marilyn watches the door in the mirror expecting it to burst open at any second all knives and blood and needles.

When it doesn't and nothing happens Marilyn says:

'You see I thought that you thought that I was a friend of yours or something and that you didn't realise that I wasn't and that I was a complete stranger and that's why I ignored you because I thought maybe you were just so out of it that you didn't care so you were just raving on like some drunk or something and not really expecting anyone to answer so that's why I didn't answer you just then.'

And then there's another pregnant menacing pause before the voice says:

'You mean sharing my innermost sense of confusion is raving on like some drunk to a complete stranger?'

207

All hurt and hysterical with tears lurking just around the corner.

And Marilyn feels the ground begin to slip away from under her feet and places one hand on the edge of the sink all pounding blood and gasping breath.

After a long pounding gasping pause Marilyn says:

'Well you know how people get in places like this and you never really know when someone's a lunatic or really out of it or an aggressive bore who's going to force you to submit to their entire life story that's ultimately going to have something to do with insurance policies do you know what I mean?'

And then the voice says:

'An aggressive bore or a nice person?' quietly and full of intense menace and madness and Marilyn hurries on in a gun-to-her-head rush:

'Right like earlier tonight just out near the bar I noticed this guy was looking at me and I must have looked back because the next thing I know he's at my elbow introducing himself as Marlon the-living-breathing-walking-talking-hard-on Brando and he seems quite nice and we chat for a bit and then he stops and it's as if the gooey plasma of our conversation suddenly squelches to a halt as he looks deeply and meaningfully into both my eyes at once and says in this smooth lilting poetic voice:

'"Wow you're really beautiful and I'd love to make you a famous film star you see I'm a film-maker and I've just made my first feature film and my father's a famous Hollywood director and has anyone ever told you seriously that you are the most beautiful creature they've ever seen on celluloid or off because I love the way you look."'

And Marilyn slowly turns around to face the cubicle and leans against the edge of the sink and thinks:

Don't shoot.

And wonders how all this is going to end.

And:

'And anyway Marlon the-living-breathing-walking-talking-hard-on Brando just goes on and on like this until I probably yawn or blink or spill the drink he bought me all down my shirt or maybe down his because all of a sudden he just stops and then he sort of clicks again and looks deeply into both my eyes at once and says in the same smooth lilting poetic voice:

'"What I'm trying to say is that talking to you just now somehow typifies the science-fiction metropolis-of-the-future nature of this crazy city do you know what I mean? But hey listen I've just noticed this friend of mine come in and if you'll wait here for me I'll be right back after I say hello and do you like blow because if you do I can get some so."

'And then he disappears and that's when I sneak away in here because even though he's incredibly good-looking he's obviously a jerk and isn't that always the case?'

And the voice says:

'Just about everyone's horrible or crazy these days.'

And then Marilyn says:

'And I don't know if I can go out there again because I don't know whether he'll sexually discriminate against me or try to rip me off or sell me drugs or mug me or molest me or what and it's really hard to tell whether people are just being friendly and nice or not and I usually just ignore people unless I know them although that's really funny that I should say that because if you knew me at all you'd know that I'm always the first to complain that there aren't any decent available intelligent well-dressed guys around because everyone's gay or married and as far as women go I never really get approached by women and if I do it's because they're crazy and maybe that's why most women I meet don't really stick or gel and they just seem to slip off or drift away or disappear into thin air or stand me up at the last minute or dematerialise into white noise or something so I spend most of my time avoiding crazies or aggressive bores or women who dematerialise into misty backdrops and in the end it doesn't really matter whether people are men or women because everyone's upstaged by their TV double anyway whether the image is Australian and so terminally infested with white noise and so many generations old that its highly suspect genealogical origin threatens to become sheerly and utterly untraceable at any minute in a random and incalculable way or whether the image is American and untouched by unidentifiable multiple-wave interferences and unimpeded by mysterious is-there-something-wrong-with-the-satellite-dish? qualities and utterly too present and too bright and too brilliant to be real.'

All the time wondering about Virginia and her too-enigmatic deeper self.

But that's when:

'Ohhhhhhhh,' another louder croakier groan oozes from the cubicle and Marilyn feels the ground turn into slippery icy slush and grips onto the sink with hard white knuckles and says all urgent concern:

'Are you all right in there like are you going to be sick

or something have you taken something you've never had before?'

But suddenly everything goes very quiet in the cubicle and Marilyn almost passes out all dizzy legs and spinning eyes and prickling sweat and so she shakes her head and bites her tongue and wonders:

Why is it that women are always almost dying on me and failing to appear deeply and enigmatically at the last minute?

And waits for the nausea to subside.

But that's when two things happen very suddenly and in quick succession which make Marilyn open her eyes and see straight because someone—

Knock knock knock—

Knocks loudly on the frosted glass panelled door and shouts:

'Hurry up in there for Christsakes! you've got three minutes ya hear me?'

And when no-one answers the voice shouts louder:

'Ya hear me?'

And that's when the second thing that happens very suddenly and in quick succession happens and the voice in the cubicle shouts:

'All right,' all gunshot and loud and Marilyn just about jumps out of her skin in shock and surprise.

And that's when Marilyn realises in a blinding neon flash of colossal magnitude that the meaning behind the words has something to do with the fact that the voice sounds very much like Virginia's voice—

Oh God Virginia—

And Marilyn wonders whether Virginia's making yet another Clayton's appearance which is much more of a disappearance or semi-apparent appearance than a straightforward cubicle confusion appearance.

So Marilyn says:

'You're all right?'

And the voice croaks and crackles back electrically:

'I'm all right.'

But Marilyn persists:

'Are you sure?'

And the voice is sure:

'Yes I'm OK.'

'OK.'

'OK.'

'Right.'

And Marilyn walks over to the frosted glass panelled door and stealthily tests the lock and makes a squinting I-should-have-known-God-I'm-an-asshole, face at the cubicle.

And then the voice who might be Virginia croaks:

'I'm not sick.'

And Marilyn says:

'You're OK.'

And the voice assures her that she's all right and that she's just feeling a bit indulgent and out of control.

And Marilyn makes another face at the cubicle although this time it's much more of a don't-make-me-laugh-Virginia sarcastic face which the voice who might be Virginia can't see and then Virginia says:

'Like I could just let go at any second and really scream you know?'

And:

'Yes.'

Marilyn knows exactly what she means.

And:

'And it's just that I know exactly how you feel

about meeting other women who don't seem to stick or gel and they just seem to slip off or drift away or disappear into thin air or stand you up or dematerialise into misty backdrops and I don't know what I'm going to do if I can't find this friend of mine because you see she didn't seem to gel or stick and somehow I ended up standing her up at the last minute and now I've come all this way looking for her and I barely even know her but I do know that we could be really close because in this really sensational spontaneous way we just simultaneously clicked deeply and enigmatically and then I ended up standing her up.'

And Marilyn is just about to say:

'Virginia?'

And Virginia is just about to say:

'Marilyn?' all Clayton's innocent sincerity when—

Bang crash pow—

A fist wrapped in a towel comes through the frosted glass panelling and starts struggling with the lock.

And then someone says:

'Oh man I can't believe this shit.'

And Marilyn leaps over the broken glass and whispers into the cubicle:

'Someone's locked us in.'

And the voice who might be Virginia whispers back:

'Someone's locked us in?'

And then the hand struggling with the lock disappears and Marilyn says:

'Someone's locked us in.'

And then the voice who might be Virginia says:

'Well I'm locked in.'

And then they shoot words at each other all fast and direct and rat-tat-tat machine-gun confusion:

'We're both locked in.'

'No I can't get out the door's stuck.'

'Which door are we talking about this one or that one?'

'This one.'

'You're kidding.'

'I'm not kidding.'

And Marilyn puts two and two together in the midst of it all and pulls on the door to the cubicle which doesn't budge and seems very stuck and then the voice says:

'See Marilyn maybe if you pull and I push OK after three one two three.'

And Marilyn shrugs:

'Sure Virginia,' and grabs onto the handle.

And then Marilyn pulls and the voice that might be Virginia pushes and on the second pull-and-push the door opens and Marilyn and Virginia both stumble to the floor and collapse in the broken glass all gasping breathless giggles and Marilyn says gushy:

'I knew it was you.'

And Virginia knows and blushes and gushes and gasps and giggles and nods.

And meanwhile a man with a pockmarked face appears at the empty panel and listens.

And Marilyn giggles and words spin from their mouths:

'. . . you disappeared . . .'

'. . . I slipped off . . .'

'. . . stood me up . . .'

'. . . didn't gel . . .'

'. . . pretending to die on me . . .'

'. . . couldn't help it . . .'

'. . . misty backdrops . . .'

'. . . didn't stick . . .'

'. . . I waited till the last minute . . .'

'. . . irresponsible . . .'

And that's when the man with the pockmarked face beneath the limp dirty blond hair that's hanging over one eye at the empty panel of the door says:

'Look guys like um the manager asked me to um see if I could convince you to co-operate and to tell you that it's kind of like if you guys don't get out of there we're going to have to call the cops I mean like why don't you just give me the keys OK?'

And Marilyn says to Virginia:

'Give him the keys.'

But Virginia doesn't seem to know what keys everyone's talking about and when the man with the pockmarked face says:

'Look I know one of you guys has got the keys.'

Virginia just shrugs and says to Marilyn:

'What keys?'

So Marilyn says:

'His keys,' and squints up her eyes and furrows her brow all—

Don't-fuck-with-me-Virginia—

And serious knowing-exactly-what's-going-on intensity.

And then Virginia sort of steps back and gives in and shrugs her shoulders and snorts through her beaky nose and says:

'How did you know?'

And Marilyn just knew but Virginia still doesn't know:

'But how?'

Although the man with the pockmarked face thinks he knows:

'Because you're crazy.'

And then Marilyn says:

'Out of control.'

And the man at the empty panel says:

'Irresponsible.'

And Marilyn says:

'Why did you do it?'

Although Virginia still doesn't seem to know what everyone else is talking about and says:

'Do what?'

All Clayton's innocent sincerity.

And that's when Marilyn has to tell her what they're talking about:

'Lock-doors-steal-keys-pretend-to-die.'

And Virginia wilts and whimpers:

'Sorry.'

And the pockmarked man looks away embarrassed and Marilyn looks down at the broken glass under the blue neon light and Virginia lets out a deep sigh like groan and goes into a long pouting stare.

But then all of a sudden Virginia looks up and smiles and says:

'Anyway Marilyn how are you?'

And gives Marilyn a fancy gift-wrapped chocolate-flavoured Statue of Liberty which makes Marilyn burst into tears which makes Virginia burst into tears and then they both wrap their arms around each other and sit there laughing and crying for a quiet little while.

i t turns out that the guy at the empty panel with the smeary pockmarked face beneath the limp dirty blond hair that hangs over one eye is called Elvis:

'Nice to meet you,' and that Elvis is the manager's brother.

And then Marilyn and Virginia help Elvis open the no longer frosted glass panelled door which takes a lot of jiggling and jaggling and wriggling of keys and then they leave all the broken glass and cubicle confusion and make tracks for the bar all tail-wagging enthusiasm and:

'God it's good to see you again.'

And:

'I can't believe this this is crazy.'

And:

'You guys must be from Ostralia huh?'

And sprout lots of silly superlatives.

Over at the Formica bar with all the coconut palms and African masks there's a lot more tail-wagging and superlative-sprouting while Marilyn introduces Elvis and Virginia to Liz and all Liz's Latino flatmates and pretty soon Elvis and Liz are talking about what they do:

'So are you film or video?'

And no Liz's not into film or video and neither's Elvis and neither of them are scriptwriters either and something warm and mysterious flashes between them like electricity.

And then Virginia says:

'So where's Marlon-the-living-breathing-walking-hard-on Brando?'

And Marilyn

the little

white shark

217

laughs because there is no Marlon the-living-breathing-walking-hard-on Brando and then Virginia laughs because it suddenly seems very funny that Marilyn made all that up on the spur of the moment and Marilyn looks very quietly pleased with herself until she sees all the angry red bumps along Virginia's arms and the backs of her hands and a menacing chord sounds in a well-cued string section somewhere and Marilyn starts thinking about oral suicide as opposed to suicide by standing knife or food poisoning or injections of illegal substances and Marilyn takes Virginia's hand and leans close to her ear and whispers in a soft mumbling voice of concern:

'What are all these red bumps?'

And Virginia laughs which makes Marilyn laugh until Virginia says:

'Mosquito bites,' which starts Marilyn thinking about being trapped in tombs full of biting mosquitoes and mummies' curses and missile displays and so Marilyn's only half laughing and wondering where Virginia fits into all this.

Meanwhile the barman joins in amongst all the coconut palms and African masks and laughs helplessly:

'Ha ha ha ha he he he he,' halfway through polishing a cocktail glass all breathless and big girlie giggles.

Although the barman's hysteria probably has more to do with the fact that it's been a quiet night and so he's been involved in a little cocktail experimentation of his own and has even had time for a quick taste of the second chef's finest Peruvian gold out in the fire escape and so his hysteria probably has a lot more to do with all this than it has to do with anything Virginia and

Marilyn might have done or said although Virginia's waving her angry spotted arm around in the air for everyone to see which looks pretty funny in itself.

And somewhere amongst all the gay abandon and mutual mirth the barman shouts them both another round because he's having such a great time and:

'It's a free country isn't it?'

And Marilyn and Virginia say:

'Thank you,' politely and stop laughing long enough to wipe the tears from their eyes.

And that's when they notice Elvis and Liz and all Liz's flatmates staring over with strange twisted smiles on their faces and empty glasses in their hands.

But as soon as Marilyn takes her first icy sip of the margarita she forgets all about their strange twisted smiles and empty glasses because something goes—

Ping—

In her head and that's when Marilyn remembers about going to Washington with Twentiethcentury:

Oh Twentiethcentury.

And then she remembers all about the familiar darting form in a very creased baggy linen suit who might have been Virginia and so while Virginia's busy clicking sensationally and spontaneously with the barman Marilyn's busy working out the connection between the mosquito bites and the tombs full of biting mosquitoes and the mummies' curses and Washington and—

Ah hah—

She's just about to ask Virginia if she's just been to Washington when Virginia suddenly turns around and slaps Marilyn on the back which causes confusion amongst Marilyn's involuntary muscles and temporarily clogs her windpipe and almost causes her to choke and she—

Cough cough—

Coughs on a little bit of icy margarita.

And Virginia keeps slapping to stop Marilyn from coughing which only makes things worse and this time there's no bottle of wine lurking around conveniently for Marilyn to guzzle and finally the barman hands Marilyn a glass of water and Virginia stops slapping and Marilyn guzzles and stops coughing and Liz and Elvis and Liz's flatmates are all staring at Marilyn and Virginia:

'Those crazy Ossies,' and shaking their heads.

By the time everything calms down a little Marilyn forgets about seeing the familiar darting form in the very creased baggy linen suit who might have been Virginia and sips silly on her drink.

And then Virginia asks Marilyn what she's been doing and Marilyn says:

'What I've been doing well it's kind of a long story.'

But so far Virginia's the first person who's asked for it and Marilyn lowers her voice to an atmospheric whisper and watches Virginia's face intently and says:

'Well you see I wait and wait for you in the departure lounge and then Lawrence turns up out of the blue and I'm not sure what he's doing there because I didn't tell him about leaving so I guess you must have seen him some time and told him I was leaving right?'

And Virginia's eyes dart down to the bar and there's an awkward silence while Virginia carefully lifts her peach margarita to her thin lips in her long lined face and—

Slurp—

Takes a noisy sip.

And the barman looks busy polishing glasses and

Marilyn starts thinking about lime pickles but stops herself just in time and doesn't care whether the barman's listening or not and whispers:

'Anyway on the flight there's this lousy hack air hostess who keeps hanging around smiling vaguely and watching over my shoulder while I try to work out how I ended up alone on a plane to New York by writing *The List of Names and Places* in a notebook I bought while I was waiting for you at the airport and anyway she ends up giving me drugs and starts to tell me her life story which is all really weird and by this time the whole Twentiethcentury thing is getting pretty exciting but then the cab driver's a real maniac and I end up hitting my head on the roof of the cab and blacking out and when I wake up outside Liz's apartment block everything's a little bit confusing again.'

And that's when Virginia says:

'So you know Twentiethcentury too?'

Which makes Marilyn suspect intuitively that Virginia already knows all about the Twentiethcentury thing and his impeccable does-he-really-work-in-Wall-Street? business suit and his appearance on the matinee show and probably already knows that Marilyn met him on her first night working as a waitress and that the whole crazy thing with the woman with those God-are-they-silicon? tits ends up in Casualty with a dozen long-stemmed reds and a note that says:

> *Dear Marilyn,*
>   *Get well soon,*
>   *Twentiethcentury S. Fox Jnr.*

221

So Marilyn squints up her eyes sexily and says:

'How do you know Twentiethcentury?'

And Virginia smiles coolly back in a deeply enigmatic very-James-Bond-girl way and says:

'Well I don't know him personally I just know him in the same way that everybody knows him you know TV shows the daily news.'

And Marilyn is almost convinced that Virginia is telling the truth which means she doesn't really know anything about Twentiethcentury yet although she's still a little suspicious after the Lawrence lime pickle incident so she stares into a hazy middle distance all the time checking Virginia's face for give-away telltale signs and murmurs:

'How did I ever meet someone like Twentiethcentury Fox in a crazy city like this of all places to meet someone like him?

'God.

'But from the moment I first saw him on that TV matinee show it was like we were two people staring at each other from different sides of a windswept street in a chilly desolate wintry cityscape.'

And then looks up at the barman who starts polishing again and Marilyn raises her eyebrows in one of those incredibly cool could-we-have-another-round-please? gestures and the barman knows exactly what she means and gets very bottle-tossing glass-spinning busy and Marilyn looks back at Virginia whose deeply enigmatic features are devoid of give-away telltale signs and whose eyes stare back roundly and innocently in a very-James-Bond-girl way from her thin lipped long lined face.

And willingly convinced of Virginia's ignorance

Marilyn rushes on to tell Virginia all about Twentieth-century and to explain how she thought Liz was Twentiethcentury's housekeeper and whispers into Virginia's ear in lots of quick sharp bursts:

'You see International Directory Assistance must have made a mistake or something which made me feel like a victim of International Directory disturbance or some kind of telecommunications refugee because I definitely asked for Twentiethcentury S. Fox the Wall Street type extraordinaire you know THE Twentiethcentury Fox and instead they just gave me Liz the Off Off Broadway hopeful and her colony of frozen cockroaches.'

And Marilyn looks over her shoulder all guilty but Liz is over on the dance floor with Elvis who's a great dancer and when she looks back Virginia's sipping on a fresh drink and the barman's back to his glasses and Marilyn notices the angry red bumps again and says:

'And what about you?'

And Virginia tries very hard to look blank but ends up looking deeply enigmatic as she scratches her arm and knits her brow half plain half pearl:

'Something came up.'

And Marilyn says:

'Something came up?'

And Virginia's knitting face says:

'A job.'

And Marilyn sighs and—

Sips—

And says:

'Doing what?' meaning what kind of job and Virginia intuits Marilyn's implicit question and unknits her brow and says:

'I can't say,' deeply and enigmatically and Marilyn says:

'You can't say?'

And then Virginia leans over and whispers very very softly:

'One day I might have to disappear completely you know really disappear in a very final and absolute way like no coming back I mean like dying you know I might have to do something final like that.'

And then there's a quiet little pause before Marilyn says:

'Oh,' not even wanting to think of the implications of Virginia's words or the consequences of everything she's just told her about Twentiethcentury if it turns out that the implications Marilyn suspects are grounded in anything like the all-too-ugly threatening truth she doesn't want to know about and sips her drink instead.

And later Elvis and Liz drag Marilyn and Virginia away to another warehouse just down the road where Liz assures them they're going to:

'Ha ha ha play ha ha golf ha ha ha,' and then rolls her eyes at Elvis who laughs loudly and rolls them back again and flaunts his tiny red capillaries and snorts a few:

'Huhs,' like Twentiethcentury although his are less gruff and snorting and more sniffling and it sounds like his sinus condition might even be worse than Twentiethcentury's especially when he says:

'Not bad for a boy from Brooklyn,' and kicks open his door.

And then they all play follow the leader up the three carpeted steps and down the long narrow hallway and crowd one after the other into the bend-your-heads-folks split-level room with a watermelon light and a PC and two milk crates and an overturned shopping trolley with no wheels covered with planks of wood and a subway map and then they all climb one after the other up the ladder to the loft and sit down on the sleeping bag on the mattress on the floor and when they're all sitting in a row under a naked bulb Elvis—

Gasp—

Cuts lots and lots of white powder with an American Express card and Marilyn begins to realise how hard it is to be herbal in this decadent decadent city where the beast lurks around every corner and maybe Twentieth-century isn't so bad after all even if he is a decadent and a fascist and a bit of a pig and definitely not the right man for her.

And so Marilyn snorts along with everyone else while Elvis explains the rules:

'Well someone stands at the bottom of the three steps with a little putting club and a plastic practice ball and they have to hit the ball up the three steps and all the way down the hallway and the idea is that you aim for the mouldy patch on the wallpaper and anyway someone else stands in front of the mouldy patch and they're like a goalie and they have to stop the ball from hitting the mouldy patch right and if the ball hits the mouldy patch well that's how you score a goal which entitles you to one more swing *comprendez*?' very very fast and everyone nods enthusiastically not really understanding and Elvis says:

'I'll go first and then you'll get the hang of it OK?'

And disappears down the ladder and Liz finishes the last crumbs of drugs and disappears after him and Elvis emerges down the long narrow corridor with a putting club and a plastic practice ball and stands down at the bottom of the three carpeted steps and takes a few wild practice swings and Marilyn and Virginia lean over the edge and watch Liz dancing around in front of the mouldy patch talking about:

'A cassette player,' and then watch mystified while she starts rummaging around the milk crates and the over-turned shopping trolley with no wheels.

And meanwhile Elvis carefully places the ball on the carpet and sways his hips from side to side and takes aim and then —

Thump —

Takes a wild swing that ends up tangled in the doorway and the ball is still sitting on the carpet and Elvis laughs and Marilyn and Virginia laugh and then:

> *Goodbye Norma Jean,*
> *Though I never knew you at all*
> *You had the grace to hold yourself*
> *While those around you crawled . . .*

And the tiny room is full of a sampled dance version of Elton John's classic pop song 'Candle in the Wind'.

But the tape's a little stretched and the song slows down and speeds up and everyone laughs as the singer's voice swells and shrinks.

And meanwhile Elvis places the ball on the carpet again and sways from side to side and then swings the club and this time the ball leaps over the three stairs and everyone holds their breath until —

Ohhhh —

It falls short of the wall and Liz darts out and tosses the ball back to Elvis and dances back to the wall to guard the mouldy patch and Marilyn turns to Virginia and says:

'This is fantastic,' and then screams down to Elvis over the music:

'I'm going next OK?'

And Elvis nods: OK.

And then places the ball on the carpet and takes aim and swings and this time he misses the ball completely and says:

'I'm a little out of practice,' mostly to himself and drops the putter.

And then Marilyn comes careering down the ladder and runs down the long narrow hallway laughing and picks up the club panting and Elvis shows her how to hold the club and then disappears up the hallway and Marilyn lines the putter up with the ball and smiles at Liz and aims at the mouldy patch and wriggles her hips and:

> *And it seems to me you lived your life*
> *Like a candle in the wind,*
> *Never knowing who to cling to*
> *When the rain set in . . .*

And then she swings wildly and the ball leaps up the three steps and makes a smooth arc down the long narrow hallway and whizzes past Liz's shoulder so Liz ducks and the ball lands smack in the middle of the mouldy patch and Marilyn leaps in the air and screams:

'Oooh eeh.'

And Virginia shouts down:

'The little white shark.'

And their eyes meet and swim smudgy blue and beady:

Marilyn's Almost Terminal New York Adventure

> *Goodbye Norma Jean,*
> *From the young man in the 22nd row*
> *Who sees you as something more than*
>   *sexual,*
> *More than just our Marilyn Monroe . . .*

And then Marilyn runs up the steps and down the long narrow hallway and throws her arms around Liz and Elvis throws his arms around them both and they all laugh and scream for a while.

And then later on when everyone's wrists are sprained from hitting the putter straight into the wall and everyone's knees are bruised from falling over trying to stop the ball from hitting the mouldy patch Virginia suggests they go back to the club to dance so everyone links arms and as they weave their way past the barman and the coconut palms and African masks to the flashing lights of the dance floor the DJ plays the latest hit from the London scene and they make a close circle and dance bumping into each other and treading on toes and Marilyn leans over to Virginia and shouts:

'There's broken glass on the dance floor.'

And Virginia rolls her eyes and smiles and Marilyn shouts:

'I'm so glad we finally met up.'

And Virginia grabs Marilyn's hand and shouts:

'What are you going to do about Twentieth-century?'

And Marilyn smiles and shouts back:

'Twentiethcentury who?'

And they both laugh and keep on dancing holding hands until Virginia shouts:

'I'm just going to the bathroom.'

And Marilyn watches Virginia disappear through the black gyrating bodies and wipes the sweat from her eyes.

And Virginia's words—

One day I might have to disappear completely—

Play over and over through her mind.

And then over at the bar with a fresh round of drinks they toast:

'To golf.'

'To dancing.'

'To New York.'

And it's only later when they stagger wet and sweaty into the icy grey lilac light in search of a cab that Liz asks Marilyn:

'What happened to Virginia?'

And Marilyn shrugs and looks away and reaches inside her overcoat and prods the now melted statue and remembers catching Virginia's eye when she'd said:

'The little white shark.'

And collapses in the back of the cab and knows deeply in her heart where it's warm and dark that she'll never see her friend again in a very final absolute kind of way and thinks that the difference between waitressing and once-in-a-lifetime employment opportunities is that sometimes once in a lifetime literally means once in a lifetime in a very literal and fatal way whereas waitressing always threatens to become terminal without actually becoming so and the thing about once-in-a-lifetime employment opportunities is that they're impossible to say no to so Marilyn is a little relieved that she's never had one yet and lying there collapsed on the back seat Marilyn sees Virginia's face on a TV screen moving in slow motion and her thin lipped long lined features are so blurred and indistinct Marilyn almost doesn't recognise her and then someone switches the TV off and Marilyn is left staring at a blank screen watching the dot shrink fade and disappear and wondering where the dot has gone.

eeeeeeeeeeeeeeeee.

Marilyn's sleeping shoulders twitch and her left arm jolts awake and her heart seems to spasm as she opens her eyes from the creaky slashed badly sprung vinyl sofa-bed in Liz's living room.

Eeeeeeeeeeeeeeeee.

And Marilyn leaps up in all the crazy bustling confusion of boxes and suitcases and stumbles through dusty gaps and staggers past seemingly secret telephones and empty picture frames and hidden light switches to the hallway where she throws herself at the intercom headset with such force that she drags it—

Oh oh—

All oozing wires from the wall—

Oh shit—

And then sighs a groggy what-day-is-it? sigh as she struggles into a giant pair of docksiders and wraps the dirty stained dust-saturated blanket around her shoulders over her father's old pyjamas.

And leaving the door slightly ajar she plunges hands outstretched and floppy flipper feet out into the peach and sage papered hallway and collapses—

Aaaah—

Just like any other slave of New York housewife in a heap in the corner of the lift.

And her eyes are so puffy she can't really see anything anyway so she closes them and then hangs her head in

just like any other

---

slave of New

York housewife

231

her hands and lets her greasy hair fall all over her face and somewhere between the seventh and eighth floors she opens her eyes again and—

Oh my God—

Finds herself peering through her hair at the oh my God that's . . . that's . . . who *is* that? movie star and—

Oh no—

And Marilyn shrinks deeper and deeper into her father's pyjamas with the ripped collar and the crutch that comes right down to her knees and the knotted drawstring that dangles over a triangle of exposed stomach flesh.

But—

Thank Christ—

The movie star doesn't seem to recognise her from behind his dark glasses and when the elevator arrives with a jolt in the lobby he mutters:

'Excuse me,' and rushes out into the snowy street.

And Marilyn counts to ten and breathes in and out slowly and thinks—

Phew—

And then peeks out into the lobby where she sees a delivery boy stomping his feet and rubbing his hands together in the cold next to a shopping trolley full of brown Food Emporium bags and Marilyn tippy-toes out and opens the door and silently beckons him towards the lift and when the doors close Marilyn gazes into his clear round long-lashed dark brown eyes and they both smile and then he helps Marilyn unload the shopping trolley and Marilyn shrugs and hands him a packet of Pepperidge Farm chocolate chip cookies instead of a tip and he just smiles and pulls down his cap and saunters off hands in pockets to the lift.

And Marilyn is just about to rip open the Pep-

232

peridge Farm whole-wheat loaf when the phone rings:

'This is Qantas airlines and we'd like to confirm your seat on Flight Q13 departing from JFK this afternoon at 3.15. p.m.'

And Marilyn says:

'Oh.'

And Qantas airlines say:

'Can I confirm your seat on Flight Q13 this afternoon?'

And Marilyn says:

'Today?'

And:

'Yes.'

Flight Q13 departs from JFK at 3.15 this afternoon and Marilyn says:

'Oh.'

And then:

'What about tomorrow?'

And Qantas airlines start to say:

'I'm sorry ma'am but at this stage we—' when Marilyn interrupts and says:

'OK.'

And Qantas airlines stop mid-sentence and say:

'Then can I confirm your seat on Flight Q13 this afternoon?'

And Marilyn says:

'Yes OK I'm in confirm me.'

And hangs up the phone more than a little stunned and amazed and sits down slowly on a dusty square of wooden floorboards with a—

Shit-a-brick—

Sigh not really convinced she's going home:

I'm going home.

233

Or really sure why she's going home at all:

I'm going home?

And everything's a bit shimmery and wobbly and dizzy and so-what's-new? confusing.

And Marilyn's just about to do something reassuring like making a cup of coffee or a Pepperidge Farm whole-wheat sandwich or taking a shower or turning on the radio when the phone rings again and that familiar no-I-never-did-have-my-adenoids-out-so-yes-I-do-have-a-sinus-condition accent says:

'Hi it's me.'

And Marilyn says:

'Hi do you have the time?'

'It's a quarter of.'

'Of what?'

'It's a quarter of eleven.'

'Oh shit.'

'What's up?'

'Twentiethcentury I'm leaving.'

'You're leaving me?'

'Leaving New York.'

'Leaving New York?'

'I'm sorry.'

And then Twentiethcentury grunts:

'Shit.'

And Marilyn can hear another phone ringing somewhere and Twentiethcentury says:

'I gotta go I'll call you back.'

And then there's a click and the dial tone and Marilyn decides to take a shower for the last time in Liz's no-longer-phenomenal sink with no plug bathroom.

And meanwhile Marilyn dreams up a quick goodbye note to Liz:

Dear Liz,

Thanks a million for everything you've done and for being such a great friend that day on the doorstep and for letting me stay and teaching me how to dance and how to make hand-blow-dried real potato French fries and I hope everything works out OK with your apartment and if you're ever in Sydney look me up and I'm sorry to leave so suddenly but I'll write and explain everything later.

Marilyn.

And by this stage Marilyn's drying carefully between each toe when the seemingly secret phone rings again:

'I'm sorry about before but I think someone just tried to kill me I mean I can't say too much about it you know for security reasons and everything but it looks like someone took a few shots at me and missed luckily huh and you'll never believe this part but the detective said that the killer is a woman.'

'What happened to her?'

'I don't know and like I don't care I mean what a fucken day and now you're leaving and I just can't get my head around it like man this is so sudden I just can't believe I'm going to walk out of here tonight and you're going to be halfway around the world I mean how far away *is* Ostralia?'

'Well it took me 31 hours to get here.'

'31 hours oh shit oh man like I've got a week's holiday coming up and I thought I could fly out for a couple of days but 31 hours.'

'I want to come back.'

'But then I guess that'd clock up a lot of mileage on my Frequent Flyers but oh man 31 hours I mean we're talking about some pretty serious air travel here.'

'I love New York I'll come back as soon as I can.'

'Oh yeah you love New York?'

'I just love walking down the streets and the snow and all the people and the museums and the clubs.'

'Oh shit I gotta go and you still haven't told me why you're leaving I mean huh look give me your number and I'll call you OK?'

'02-331-2632.'

'Because huh I think we're onto something pretty serious here.'

'Yeah.'

'OK Marilyn my little Ossie girl.'

'Bye Twentiethcentury.'

'This is stupid like I miss you already.'

'You do?'

'I love you.'

'Do you?'

'I've gotta go.'

'OK.'

'Bye.'

'Bye.'

And:

Click.

And Marilyn sighs in French into an empty picture frame and wonders why she suddenly feels like some kind of rare deadly psychologically disturbed jellyfish and shakes her head.

And then Marilyn writes Liz's quick goodbye note and slips into her jeans and a white T-shirt and her 100% cotton socks and black patent lace ups and—

Yes—

Virginia's chocolate statue is still in the inside pocket of her overcoat and has hardened up nicely and God only knows where Virginia has disappeared to now but Marilyn just doesn't even want to start thinking about that and then it's—

Ciao—

To the colony of frozen cockroaches and out into the cold snowy street.

And everything's one big—

Rush rush rush—

Up to the subway on 53rd and just as she's crossing the corner of 51st and Lex. against the lights she—

Whoosh—

Slips in the slushy snow and lands flat on her back in all the dirty mush:

Whoops.

'Are you all right lady?'

And Marilyn just giggles breathlessly and blushes and the lights change and the cab driver smiles and drives off and Marilyn picks herself up and tries to brush off the brown mush but gives up in a frantic panic stricken I've-got-a-plane-to-catch hurry.

And just as she's squelching into the steaming depths of the subway station she comes face to face with a well-preserved in a very blue-eyed blonde-haired big-busted sort of way Upper East Side ageing nameless movie star who's probably on her way up to Bloomies and an appointment with her therapist before a quick stop at that deli on the Upper West Side that everyone's talking about on her way home to meet her does-he-still-work-on-Wall Street? businessman and for a second or two the four gold-flecked smudgy blue eyes meet and swim in a chilly heart-stopping pool of recognition:

Touché.

One pair almost smiling and relieved and the other impersonating a blank canvas beneath layers of whale blubber and powder.

And then suddenly the crush rushes on and Marilyn's washed away and deposited at the end of the queue for subway tokens that seems to wind on forever so she breathes a deep reckless breath and makes a run for it and leaps over the turnstiles in a single bound and squelches all the way down the escalator and pushes her way to the front of the platform as the E train rushes in and a muffed furry-hatted scarved goggled man says:

'Last night I hat a dream zat I vas back in Siberia.'

And Marilyn decides not to ask him how to get to the airport as she forces her way through the thick damp woolly bodies:

'Stand clear of the closing doors please,' and onto the crowded E train.

And Marilyn can't understand anything else the guard is saying and then she gets pressed so tightly against the closed doors that she's too terrified to blink let alone ask directions and thinks a silent prayer:

Please God don't let me end up in the Bronx.

And somewhere past Grand Central she hears that no-I-never-did-have-my-adenoids-out-so-yes-I-do-have-a-sinus-condition accent as it grunts gruffly from somewhere inside the car:

'You see Fonda huh the man in the street don't know shit that's why he's in the street ha ha.'

But no it isn't Twentiethcentury and Marilyn gradually

worms her way over to a subway map and devises a plan of action and people eventually squeeze:

'Excuse me,' in and out of the car but mostly out of the car and Marilyn squeezes out at Washington Square and searches desperately for the way to the JFK line and runs blindly through the tunnels like a rat in a maze with the cries of Manhattan the beast ringing in her ears.

And on the next platform hurry-up-I've-got-a-plane-to-catch Marilyn stands next to a man in a tea cosy who mutters:

'Whenever I lose money I feel like killing myself,' over and over and tries not to stare.

Inside the next carriage a guy in a pink furry coat is singing homemade rap music and rolling a stick of hash between his palms and then he says to no-one in particular:

'Man if they'd legalise this stuff crack would stop.'

And a woman in a red plastic hat croaks back:

'They could tax it too.'

And Marilyn tries not to wonder about the time or whether she'll miss the plane.

And meanwhile she stares at a sprayed message that says:

You are what you eat
You were what you shit.

While Twentiethcentury's gruffly grunted words play over and over in her mind.

'**m**um it's me.'
'Marilyn where are you?'
'I'm in LA.'

'Your father and I have been so worried about you we've been phoning your flat for a week and no-one seems to know where you are and Lawrence said something about America and we've been so worried with all the gang murders and everything.'

'Mum that was in Washington and I've been—'

'I just don't understand how you could just go off like that.'

'Mum—'

'You've no idea have you your father and I have been worried sick about you I can feel a bout of pneumonia coming on and your father's heart has taken a turn for the worst.'

'Mum I'm coming home.'

But somehow home doesn't feel like home any more and Marilyn wonders where home is as she wanders the neon labyrinthine tunnels of LA International Airport.

And by the time she squeezes into another lots-of-extra-leg-room emergency exit seat the tears are already pouring silently down each cheek and Marilyn tries to ignore the red-haired bespeck-

all of a sudden

words seem to

leap out and

speak themselves

led freckled man in the next seat until he says:

'I always find it's best to you know just let it all out.'

And Marilyn wipes her eyes and sighs jerky sighs while the serious sinus sufferer's squeaky voice continues:

'You know Marilyn I know just what you're going through you see I always wanted to be a film-maker and I think if I made films I'd make them like Ingmar Bergman you know and yet here I am an unknown jazz clarinettist all full of craziness and obscure yearnings and neuroses and complexities and I've never been able to tell anyone except my analyst about my three broken marriages and breakdown but that's because here look do you want my nuts I never eat peanuts my doctor says they give you cancer so—'

And Marilyn sobs thanks and gobbles down the peanuts and the serious sinus sufferer's squeaky voice whines on and on so Marilyn nods and ums for a while until a little light goes—

Ping—

Inside her head.

And that's when Marilyn opens up her purchased-just-prior-to-departure now-I'm-going-to-keep-a-travel-diary notebook and she's just in the middle of the bit about her dream about being mugged by an elephant in Central Park when she glimpses a familiar form hovering nervously just behind her and she turns around just in time to catch Bette the lousy hack air hostess leaning over her shoulder and reading from *The List of Names and Places* but instead of looking embarrassed or apologising or dematerialising into a misty backdrop Bette just offers her hand and says:

'Hi Marilyn I'm Bette I've been hearing so much

about you and I've been dying to meet you again remember we met last week?' all flaring nostrils and wildly staring eyes and Marilyn nods blankly and lets Bette shake her limp soggy-napkins hand and then Bette smiles all sugar and spice and disappears.

And Marilyn spends the rest of the flight locked in a tiny tinny toilet cubicle trying to work out who Bette is and where she's been that she's been hearing all about her and where she fits into *The List of Names and Places* and gets no sleep at all and subsists solely on Virginia's chocolate Statue of Liberty which she sucks slowly and deliciously in a corner of her mouth.

And Marilyn only ventures out again when the Captain announces that they're just about to arrive at Sydney airport and when she gets back to her seat the jazz clarinettist looks up and smiles from his book on psychoanalysis and dreams and whines squeakily:

'I know just what you're going through because I used to find flying an intensely frightening and traumatic experience and like I used to be just like you locking myself in toilets nauseous with paranoia and all those screaming children but that was before I started therapy and . . .' and on and on and so on.

And Marilyn looks out the window where Sydney's northern beaches come into view beneath the white fluffy clouds and while crispy cicada shells and Christmas beetles all sing a song of joy through the echoing tunnels of her intestines Marilyn's momentarily blinded by a flash of that other city and Manhattan the beast winks goodbye at her with one of its thousand invisible eyes through all the steamy fog and grey mist and for a very quick second Marilyn feels as if she's going to cry again but she doesn't.

And then—

Wow—

The plane breaks through the fluffy white into bright blue sunshine over the twinkling turquoise ripples of Botany Bay and then touches down onto the smooth cement runway and taxis into the gate and Marilyn laughs out loud when the men in the yellow stubbies and long knee socks spray the plane with tall aerosol cans of keep-the-bugs-away-from-our-clean-golden-shores insecticide which causes the unknown jazz clarinettist to make a lot of choking and coughing noises and meanwhile everything seems too bright and too sunny as they both sit laughing in the sunny Sydney glare.

And later the unknown jazz clarinettist asks in his serious sinus sufferer's squeaky voice:

'So what do you do?'

And for a few seconds Marilyn's mind goes blank and she squints up her eyes sexily and stares off into a hazy middle distance and she's just about to give the usual condensed encapsulated reply when all of a sudden words seem to leap out and speak themselves and *The List of Names and Places* rises up like a vision and Marilyn moves her motormouth and says:

'I write lists.'

And the a-writer-really-oh-how-fascinating-that's-wonderful-a-writer? unknown jazz clarinettist introduces himself as:

'Woody.'

And Marilyn says:

'Oh,' and sighs a brisk whisky: isn't-he-Woody-Woody-what's-his-name? sigh.

And then they stumble down the long conveyor

belts and through customs and Marilyn peers through the brown sliding doors half expecting to see hairy snail Lawrence waving from the other side and then Woody-Woody-what's-his-name squeaks:

'Would you like to share a cab I mean if you're meeting someone you'll probably want to go home with them I mean in their car back to your place I mean back to their place I mean but if you're not then I can drop you off somewhere or maybe we can go back to my hotel for a drink or a coffee just to recover if you know what I mean.'

And Marilyn follows him out to the taxi stand as he stumbles and trips with his creaking bulging suitcase.

And just as Woody drops his bag:

'Oh damn,' with a seam-splitting screech spilling neatly folded piles of white boxer shorts and boxes of freshly laundered pale blue shirts and baggy khaki cotton drill trousers all over the butt-splattered pavement Marilyn catches a glimpse of Lawrence's just-like-a-B-grade-actor-playing-a-flawed-hero-in-a-low-budget-third-rate-Hollywood-Disaster-Movie faded-denim form and it's in a kind of neon flash of colossal magnitude that she recognises Bette the lousy hack air hostess—

Wow—

As she nuzzles Lawrence's neck:

So that's where Bette fits into The List of Names and Places.

And Marilyn shakes her head and shakes her head again and shrugs and gulps away the dry blood taste in the back of her throat and watches Lawrence and Bette disappear through the shimmering glare into the car park.

And then Marilyn turns to her red-haired bespeckled freckled friend and says:

'So how did you know my name's Marilyn?'

And Woody-Woody-what's-his-name looks up from the pavement and says:

'Well I don't know I guess you just look like a Marilyn with all your blonde hair and your beautiful blue eyes.'

And Marilyn kneels down and helps him repack his broken bag and they smile shyly at each other through pairs of sore squinting eyes.

dear Marilyn,
Go ahead blow me off I can take it.
I guess Wall Street types tend to be loners and
I'm used to it.

But I can't help thinking about you
coming back you know?

Are you coming back?

I mean what the fuck's going on here?

I mean I thought we were onto a pretty
important deal here but every time I call
you there's no answer.

I'd write you a poem but I'm not even
sure if this is the right address.

Anyway I'd still really appreciate that
list you know? Even if you don't come
back because like what's the point of
paying all those fees for a personal attorney if
you never take their advice? And you never
can tell these
days.

Let me know what you're doing either way.	**never say no**
Regards, Twenti- ethcentury.	**to adventures**
PS I know you're a heartreak- er but don't	**even when**
fuck with me Marilyn	**they threaten to**
	become terminal

*because you haven't dealt with a New York
broken heart before and I don't think you
want to like there's a lot of things you
don't know about me Marilyn and there's a
lot of things you probably wouldn't want
to know if I told you but just for starters
you don't even know my real name but if you
want to know and you think you can
handle it then how about accepting one of my
very expensive desperately lust-filled long
distance telephone calls for a change huh?*
                    'Twentiethcentury S. Fox Jnr'

And Marilyn shakes her head in mild disgust and
refolds Twentiethcentury so-that's-why-you-wanted-that-
list-of-everybody-I've-ever-slept-with Fox's letter full of
I'm-just-going-to-have-to-call-your-bluff-big-boy   and
what-are-you-going-to-do-kill-me-because-I-don't-love-
you-any-more? outrage and puts the letter back in her
pocket and wonders with a desultory sigh whether it
has all been worth it.

But Marilyn can't quite get her head around the
question so she imagines that she's being interviewed
about her recent trip to New York on television by a
recently-resurrected-from-the-obscurity-of-low-ratings-
by-incarceration-in-a-twelve-step-program   host   and
Marilyn imagines that the host would get all the way to
the end of the interview before fixing her with his
sleazy gaze and asking in a coy predictable TV personality
way the question everyone's been waiting to hear:

*So Marilyn given the broad scope of everything
you've told us tonight given all the ups and downs the
highs and lows the heady glories and the heavy blows*

given all the ins and outs the twists and turns the spec-
tacular crashes and the giddy upwards curves given all
this, what would you say Marilyn if I were to tell you that
it was possible to go right back to the beginning again
and start all over would you do it would you do it all
again?

And the camera would zoom in for a close-up of
Marilyn's face and everybody watching TV all over the
world would think how her face is very Marilyn-with-a-
touch-of-Meryl and Marilyn would smile and frown in a
thoughtful so-this-is-really-it way and then stare
directly into the camera and say:

Never neglect a girlfriend in your pursuit of a
boyfriend because men are never as significant as they
look and women are inevitably more so but most
important of all never say no to adventures even when
they threaten to become terminal because you never
can tell how things will turn out in the end and even if
everything turns out to be a total here-we-go-again-
you-can-say-bye-bye-to-your-sanity disaster it doesn't
seem to matter because everything's always OK
anyway and even if you end up feeling like the biggest
loser in history you'll still end up feeling like something
and something isn't that bad no matter how nothing it
seems.

And the recently resuscitated host would look titillated
and reluctantly amused and would raise one eyebrow and
would be just about to ask Marilyn to clarify her position
when there would be an interruption in transmission
and the screen would buzz in a brilliant virtuoso of
white noise.

And Marilyn guesses that her answer to the recently
resuscitated host's timely question means yes she

would do it all again and this makes her very excited:

Yippee!

And she's just about to ring hairy snail Lawrence and begin again when she realises she can't because he's with Bette now so she thinks some more and she's just about to ring Miller when she realises she can't because his wife will probably answer the phone so she calls Durrell instead but the phone just rings and rings unanswered and Marilyn wonders why he doesn't buy an answering machine and then the phone cuts out and she can't ring Virginia because Virginia's probably dead or something worse and she sighs and sits staring at the blank screen of her small portable TV thinking lots of the-party's-over and that's-all-folks thoughts when suddenly she remembers that she can watch TV now without sneezing so she switches on the TV and stares in the general direction of the screen but she can't tell whether it's on or off or if she's sitting too close or too far away because no matter where she sits or how she twists the switch the screen remains a dark grey blur and definitely doesn't look like a TV should especially when the program says she's watching a documentary on the Kennedys and soon a whole lot of thoughts whizz around in her head like:

I thought JFK was better looking.

And:

Doesn't he look a little too dishevelled and world-weary to be the President of the United States?

And that's when even more disturbing thoughts start to whizz around like:

He looks incredibly like like like—

And even worse:

Oh my God is that Virginia standing over there

250

next to Lee Harvey Oswald?

But in the end the dark grey blur makes the images altogether too too obscure and wondering about Virginia is far too exhausting and everything she thinks about Twentiethcentury is very silly and soon she lets go of everything that's lurking and whizzing about inside her mind and slips into la la land which is when she starts to feel very very nice and very very alone and even a tiny bit terminal.

And while it may be difficult for most readers to understand how Marilyn is feeling at this specific point in time because feeling a tiny bit terminal is very tricky and quite difficult to imagine given the degree of incongruity involved Marilyn is undoubtedly capable of experiencing such a bizarre sensation precisely because it really and truly isn't her idea at all and that's because it's most probably and almost certainly and—

You better believe it—

Mine.

You see I think I've been very good about all of this and everything that's happened so far keeping very quiet and aloof and in the background but now it's my turn to have my say and:

Yes, I am upset that Marilyn's feeling this way and:

No, I'm not altogether happy about it.

And I'm still feeling unhappy about Marilyn's tiny bit terminal state of mind when she suddenly evaporates from her chair and then passes straight into the television screen in a totally inconceivable did-that-really-happen? kind of way:

Wow.

And I have no idea whether Marilyn is dead or alive or if she's been reinvented as a soap star or a writer or whether she'll ever come back as the Marilyn she once was although I can't help noticing that her purchased-just-prior-to-departure now-I'm-going-to-keep-a-travel-diary notebook isn't the only thing she left behind and that lying right beside it on the grimy carpeted floor is an almost invisible lock of her fabulously blonde hair which is just as well because while Twentiethcentury is certain to seize her notebook when he turns up to get things straight between them in a very final way as he is sure to do any day now he's unlikely to notice her almost invisible lock of hair and while this outcome is not untouched by a certain desolate windswept inevitability it's also extremely lucky for Marilyn in a Hollywood sequel kind of way and bodes well for her future indeed.

Justine Ettler
The River Ophelia

Justine loves Sade.

And Justine is out of control . . .

Set in a world of inner-city grunge bars and clubs, kinky
sex, drug-taking and desperation, *The River Ophelia*
explores the uncharted waters of female desire, where
the roles of victim and victimised blur and shift. Both an
homage to and subversion of de Sade's *Justine* and
Shakespeare's *Hamlet*, it is an explicit account of sexual
obsession and violence.

In the tradition of Bret Easton Ellis and Kathy Acker,
Justine Ettler's novel breaks new ground, and will
electrify, shock and provoke.

'. . . its combination of inner-urban night life and wider
cultural reference suggests nothing so much as a
marriage between Helen Garner and the Marquis de
Sade . . . Justine Ettler may be Sydney's Empress of
Grunge'
AUSTRALIAN BOOK REVIEW

'. . . a violent and unredeemed vision of life in Australia's
inner cities'
CANBERRA TIMES

John O'Brien
Leaving Las Vegas

The first novel by John O'Brien, *Leaving Las Vegas* is a disturbing and emotionally wrenching story of a woman who embraces life and a man who rejects it. Sera, a prostitute, and Ben, an alcoholic, stumble together and discover in each other a respite from their unforgiving lives. A testimony to the raw talent of its young author, who tragically committed suicide in 1994, *Leaving Las Vegas* is a compelling story of unconditional love between two disenfranchised and lost souls – an overlooked classic.

'A brutal and unflinching portrait of the low life in the city of high rollers, *Leaving Las Vegas* is both shocking and curiously exhilarating. John O'Brien was a stunningly talented writer who created poetry from the most squalid materials. This is a beautiful and horrifying novel'
JAY MCINERNEY, AUTHOR OF *BRIGHTNESS FALLS*

'Here is that rarest jewel, a really fine novel.
John O'Brien has a very great talent'
LARRY BROWN, AUTHOR OF *BIG BAD LOVE*

'This book is not only dark and dire, it is crushing . . .
Leaving Las Vegas is the strongest and most extreme look at alcohol I've ever read'
RON CARLSON, AUTHOR OF *PLAN B FOR THE MIDDLE CLASS*

Hugh Mackay
Little Lies

From Australia's foremost social commentator comes a novel of deception and intrigue, told in three voices. Three voices, three stories . . . but who can you trust?

Cole's story:
Modesty and humility don't get you far in this business, I'm afraid. No, let me be more candid: modesty and humility can be great assets, as long as you don't let them stand in the way of your ambition . . . and I never did.

Georgina's story:
I sometimes wonder whether Cole is actually the sort of man who needs the tension of having two women after him at once . . . it seemed to keep him under control, in a funny kind of way.

Keith's story:
What do you make of Cole's extraordinary behaviour at the cemetery? Blood on his hands? Would you say? You wouldn't. Neither would I. Too melodramatic. Way off the mark. Truth would be nastier than that.

Little Lies is a brilliantly controlled, blackly funny novel from the bestselling author of *Reinventing Australia* and *Why Don't People Listen?*

Peta Spear
Sex Crimes

Slade blows smoke rings and asks, 'Are you afraid?'
   'No.'
   'Even if I was in love with you?'
   'No.'
   'Why do you want me to hurt you?'
   'Why are you in love with me?'

That summer Slade met Luce and things exploded
between them. In the heavy tropical heat each seems
able to satisfy the deepest needs in the other. But Luce
wants to push further, beyond mere desire.

Sex, desire, love, eroticism . . . in this collection of
stories, Peta Spear's sensual, haunting prose explores
moments of intense passion – and dark obsession.

Billie Love, phone sex worker, gets a private line for a
special client – her lover; Lena initiates Nino into the
pleasures of the invisible gaze from the building
opposite; Michaela draws the very essence of her lover
into her art . . .

Lush, searing, driven, *Sex Crimes* announces the arrival
of a blazing new talent.

No-one has written about love like this before.